RIDERS OF RIFLE RANGE

During his first three months as a
veterinarian in Scrub Pine town, Jeff
Jones had encountered antagonism,
prejudice, and ignorance among the
feuding cattlemen and farmers. He
did not like open warfare! And open
warfare was there on Scrub Pine
grass. When Doc Jeff diagnosed a
sick bull on the Endicott ranch
as having the contagious blackleg
disease, he got involved in the
warfare — whether he liked it
or not!

SPECIAL MESSAGE TO READERS

WADE HAMILTON

RIDERS OF RIFLE RANGE

Complete and Unabridged

LINFORD
Leicester

First published in the
United States of America

First Linford Edition
published 1997

Copyright © 1970 by Wade Hamilton

British Library CIP Data

Hamilton, Wade, *1910* –
    Riders of rifle range.—Large print ed.—
Linford western library
    1. American fiction—20th centur
    2. Large type books
    I. Title
    813.5′2 [F]   LP

    ISBN 0–7089–7988–2

Published by
F. A. Thorpe (Publishing) Ltd.
Anstey, Leicestershire

Set by Words & Graphics Ltd.
Anstey, Leicestershire
Printed and bound in Great Britain by
T. J. Press (Padstow) Ltd., Padstow, Cornwall

This book is printed on acid-free paper

1

DISSATISFACTION glistened in Jeff Jones's blue eyes as he watched Endicott brand the yearling bull. As the hot iron burned through shaggy red hair, smoke lifted, a ribbon of gray against the sunlight.

"You're burning that brand awful deep, Endicott."

The rancher did not look up. When he pulled back the branding iron, the bull bawled in pain.

"That makes him my critter for sure, Doc," the rancher told Jeff Jones. "Wonder how come my riders missed him in spring-brandin' roundup?"

"You run over an awful big territory, Endicott."

"That I do," the rancher agreed. One of Endicott's men was cranking the handle of the forge over by the blacksmith shop. Ignoring Jeff Jones,

1

the rancher called to the hand: "Give me a lift, Jim?"

Doctor Jeff Jones felt the first touch of anger. Rancher Endicott had deliberately not asked him for help in untying the branded bull. To conceal his anger, the veterinarian looked across the sloping, dried Montana hills at the gray sagebrush and greener greasewood.

"Be right over, boss," the cowpuncher hollered.

"We'll dehorn him first." Doc Jeff noticed the deliberate belligerency in Endicott's voice. "Come fall, he'll be a nice chunk of fat Hereford beef."

Doc Jeff said, "Sure, if he isn't dead."

The vet saw blood flush the suntanned jowls of the rancher. Still, Endicott kept his eyes on the bull.

"He won't kick the bucket, Doc."

"He has blackleg disease."

Endicott was as stubborn as a bronc. "You say he has blackleg, and I say he ain't. There ain't no blackleg germs on my range, Doc, and you know it."

"There's a first time for everything, Endicott," Doc Jeff pointed out.

Endicott shook his head doggedly. "This bull ain't got no blackleg disease."

Doc Jeff felt futility rise in him, but such a feeling was not new to him. For three months now, he had practiced his profession on Scrub Pine range. After graduating from the 'cow college,' he had moved to Scrub Pine town and hung out his shingle as a veterinarian.

During those three months, he had encountered the maximum of antagonism, prejudice, and ignorance. He had jumped at the chance when the Dean of Veterinary Sciences had told him of an opening at Scrub Pine. For Doc Jeff, having been born and reared on a Colorado cow outfit, liked open range. But he did not like open warfare! And open warfare it was, here on Scrub Pine grass.

He had been in his office, down in Scrub Pine town, when the youngest

Endicott boy had entered and asked him to come to the Endicott ranch to look at the bull. His mother had sent him and had asked that Doc Jeff come without Mike Endicott's knowledge.

Big Mike Endicott was a stubborn man. Through hard work and tenacity, he had turned his Quarter Circle U cow outfit into one of Montana's biggest spreads. What he lacked in brains he made up for in tenacity. Endicott had not allowed Doc Jeff to vaccinate the bull. Instead, he had branded the sick animal, and now he intended to dehorn him. Both of these acts would weaken the bull considerably at a time when the animal's illness demanded all his strength.

Doc Jeff knew that blackleg was indeed a serious disease. Within a few days, blackleg could diminish the number of cattle, especially the young stock.

The symptoms were simple. First, the shoulders got stiff and rigid; then the skin became brittle. Also, the skin under

4

the hair turned a blue-black color, thereby giving the dreaded disease its name.

Jeff knew that all of the Quarter Circle U young stock — the bull plus all steers, and heifers under a year old — should be immediately vaccinated. He had mentioned this to Mike Endicott, but had met strong opposition. Endicott had claimed, rather harshly, that he had run cattle on this Scrub Pine range for almost twenty-five years. There had never been any blackleg germs on this range! There were none now. Why should there be any now?

Jeff had pointed out that farmers, when they brought in strange stock, might have also brought in blackleg germs. At the mention of the word 'farmers,' Mike Endicott had cursed in no uncertain terms.

Farmers! Hang the farmers! They were squatting on his land, stringing barbed wire across his range, building ditches and plowing his virgin soil, ruining his cattle range!

Now Doc Jeff squatted beside the bull and ran his fingers through the mass of curly, wet red hair. Endicott watched him in sullen silence.

"Did you hear that little crackling sound, Endicott?"

Endicott had heard it. Still he shook his head, stubborn to the core.

"Never heard no sound, Jeff."

Doc Jeff kept his head down to hide his anger. Again he ran his fingers through the bull's hair, pressing them down harder this time on the hot hide, then pulling them across the bull's shoulder.

"You heard it then, didn't you?"

Endicott got to his feet. "Doc Jeff, you got a heck of a good imagination, and you know it!" He spat tobacco juice into the corral dust. "You got a better imagination than you have ears." Then the rancher spoke to the cowpuncher who had come over to stand beside him. "Jim, we gotta give this bull the works. When we get done with him he won't be a bull . . . he'll be a steer — castrated, branded, an' dehorned."

Doc Jeff stood up slowly and wiped his hands on his pants. He was twenty-four, bony and tall, not too good looking. His jaws and cheeks were flat and sloping, and his nose was slightly hawkish, separating two blue eyes — blue eyes that could, on occasion, harden very quickly, and, on another, dance and laugh. Just now, though, there was no laughter in them.

"You didn't want to hear that sound, Mike Endicott!"

Endicott grinned to hide his anger. "Heck, Doc, my ears are good! This bull ain't got blackleg, fella. Shootin' serum in him would be a waste of time. Fergit it, Doc."

"Blackleg is contagious. Other cattle will get it. It should be stopped here and now."

"Fergit it, for Gawd's sake, Doc Jeff!"

The cowpuncher, anxious to avert outright trouble, offered, "Let's git to work, boss."

Doc Jeff Jones, hiding his futility, shrugged. Further conversation, he realized, was useless. He went to the pump for a cold drink of water and was working the wooden handle when Mike Endicott's wife, Clara, came out the back door of the two-story ranch house.

Mrs. Endicott was a heavy-set, matronly woman who was very near-sighted. Despite her defect, she would not wear glasses. Now she peered at Doc Jones.

"What happened, Doc Jeff?"

"He's right stubborn, Mrs. Endicott."

"How well I know that, sir. Did you vaccinate the bull?"

"He wouldn't let me."

She blinked her watery eyes, giving this information some attention. She had reared five of Mike Endicott's children, but she had only the two youngest — two boys — at home.

Somehow, she reminded Doc Jeff of a gopher gingerly poking his head out of his hole, all the time being slightly afraid of what he sees. But Clara Endicott was a good wife and a better mother, with a kind and sympathetic heart.

Now she seemed to be talking to herself. Jeff, listening to her words, lifted his cup and drank of the clear, cold water.

"So he wouldn't let you vaccinate, eh? Mike is a good man, honest and square, but so stubborn! And he always means well, too." Again her eyes peered at him. "How does a person put the vaccine in a critter, Doctor Jeff?"

Jeff Jones almost smiled. To be called 'doctor' still made him feel a little embarrassed. Besides being a 'horse doctor,' he also had to serve as a medical doctor sometimes, for there was no M.D. in Scrub Pine.

He explained carefully how one vaccinated a critter. The operation, he said, was simple. You merely inserted a hypodermic needle into the shoulder of the animal, being careful to get the needle between the hide and the flesh.

"You have to insert the needle on a slant, like this." He demonstrated. "You grab the hide, quickly insert the needle, and then push down on the plunger. But first, of course, you fill the plunger from the bottle of vaccine — like this, Mrs. Endicott."

The matron looked around, fearful that ears might be listening. "I could vaccinate that bull myself."

"You sure could. It isn't hard to do."

Again she seemed to be conversing with herself. Her weak eyes blinked, and her lips moved slowly.

"My husband will tie the bull in the barn. He'll keep him under his eye for a few days. But if the bull lives, my husband will get a secret satisfaction out of proving you were wrong, Doctor Jones."

"The main thing, Mrs. Endicott, is to save the bull."

10

"Will you leave a needle and syringe and some vaccine with me?"

"I sure will. That bull is valuable. Besides, blackleg has to be stopped or thousands of cattle will die."

"Are you sure the bull has blackleg?"

Doc Jeff was very sure. If the bull were not vaccinated, he would die within forty-eight hours, maybe less. Of course, if Mrs. Endicott secretly vaccinated the bull and saved his life, Mike Endicott, ignorant of the vaccination, would spread the news that the new vet had been wrong.

But Doc Jeff put these thoughts aside; the bull's life was what counted, not his reputation as a vet.

"Where are the implements I'm to use, Doctor?"

"They're in my bag, tied to my saddle. I'll lead my horse around the back and pretend I'm going to give him a drink at the water trough. That way, we'll be hidden from the corral, and your husband can't see us."

"I'll meet you there."

Doc Jeff's horse was tied to the corral. When he returned, Mike Endicott and his hired hand were still working on the bull. As Jeff untied his blood bay, Endicott looked up, a scowl on his rugged face.

"Leavin', Doc?"

"Sure am, Mike."

"Good-bye, Doc."

"Got to water my horse yet," Doc Jeff said.

Mike Endicott returned to his task, and Jeff led the bay around to the trough. He had three syringes in his bag. He filled one with vaccine from the sealed bottle and gave it to Mrs. Endicott.

"I'll vaccinate him, Doctor Jeff."

"Good luck."

Doc Jeff swung into his saddle lightly and loped past the corral until he was out of sight in the high cottonwood trees. Unknown to him, Mike Endicott had watched him leave, and now the cowman pulled his sleeve across his sweaty forehead and spat in the dust.

"That doc is a good young fellow," he told his hired hand. "By all rights, he should be mad at me, but when he rode past here, he waved and smiled. Right nice fellow, the doc."

2

DOC JONES left the Quarter Circle U ranch at a long, trail-eating lope, the muscles of his bay powerful under his saddle. Now anger had left him, and once again he was normal — boyish, grinning with a devil-be-hanged attitude. Maybe he was happy because he was thinking of Millicent Simmons.

Just a week ago, Millicent had opened the Branding Iron Cafe, in Scrub Pine. Doc Jeff Jones could see her again — red coils of lovely hair, blue eyes clear as the Montana skies and a peaches-and-cream complexion to match, and a stubby, short nose, dotted with a few freckles. And could she cook! It was enough to make a man want to propose to her!

She was the niece of a farmer who had homesteaded on Clear Creek, four

14

miles from Scrub Pine toward the western mountains. She had not stayed long on her uncle's farm, for she had saved a few dollars of her own, having worked in a restaurant in Illinois before coming to Scrub Pine. She had also borrowed money from the bank, so Doc Jeff had heard, and then opened the cafe.

Doc Jeff had not tried very hard to get into Millicent's favor. For one thing, he was very busy; besides, he was in no hurry. But the night before, a tent show had visited Scrub Pine, and Millicent had attended the festivities with Matt Wheeler.

Jeff had not liked that one bit. Matt Wheeler was the local land-locater. His job was to place farmers on homesteads, and for this he charged a fee — one hundred dollars per farmer, which was far too much. Doc Jeff knew this, as did the local residents, but the farmers who were greenhorns, were unaware that Matt Wheeler was cheating them.

Getting land free from Uncle Sam

had warped the farmers' judgment. They could have located wherever they wanted; then they could have merely notified the county surveyor, who would have surveyed the boundaries of the homesteads they wanted free of charge. The homesteader had only to file his first claim papers, live on his property, and make certain improvements, such as building a cabin.

But the farmers were greenhorns from big Eastern cities. And, of course, Matt Wheeler had a homestead of his own; in this manner, he convinced settlers that he, too, was a homesteader. He had even hired a man, apparently a surveyor, to establish boundaries, and for this he charged another fee.

The hired man's name was Lee Osborne. A short, squat man who perpetually scowled, he packed two six-shooters. For the first time, Jeff saw a surveyor who had need not for one six-gun, but for two.

At the tent show last night, Matt

Wheeler, beaming and elegantly garbed, had had hold of Millicent's arm, escorting her toward the choice seats. Jeff had asked her to go with him. She had said he had been too late. He had, of course, accepted this in good faith. Being a gentleman, he had not asked who was to escort her to the gala affair.

Now, loping toward town and his office, he remembered how his eyes had met those of Matt Wheeler, how Wheeler had gloated. He and Wheeler had not had trouble to date, but between them lay a thin veil of antagonism that could be easily lifted.

He was now riding through the lava-rock country a few miles out of town. Already the afternoon had changed to dusk — a tawny darkness that clung to these black badlands. Here, nature, in boiling grandeur, had in prehistoric days tumbled molten lava out of the earth's cracks, and this lava had cooled to create gaunt spires and other freaks of nature.

But the farmers had cut a wagon road through the lava. Occasionally, there was a point where the road had been widened so that two wagons could meet or pass. The road ran about a mile through the lava beds, then lifted its solitary way over a hill before slanting down and becoming a part of Scrub Pine's main street.

As Doc Jeff neared a wide spot, a rider suddenly moved out of the black rocks and stationed his horse in the middle of the road. The sudden appearance of the rider emerging from behind the huge black rocks was uncanny, it happened so quickly.

Startled, Doc Jeff reined in his bay, then recognized the rider as Matt Wheeler. He instinctively looked around for Lee Osborne, for Wheeler never traveled without him. But for once it seemed that Lee Osborne was nowhere in sight. Jeff returned his gaze to Wheeler, who was riding a black bronc, deliberately blocking the road.

"Do you need the whole trail, Wheeler?"

Wheeler smiled, a tight, ugly smile, and moved a little in his saddle. He had deliberately shifted his body so that his right hand was directly over the holstered .45, which Jeff quickly noticed. It told him trouble was ahead.

Again the vet glanced into the rocks, scanning them for some sign of Osborne. It did not seem logical that Wheeler would ride out alone. But he saw no sign of the gunman.

"I asked you a question, Wheeler! Do you need all of the road?"

Now Wheeler spoke. He had a rough, deep voice. "Shore I do, mister. Were you just out to doctor a sick bull at the Endicott spread? Were you, cow doc?"

"Cow doc, eh?"

"I asked you the question! Answer it, vet!"

Doc Jeff said, "Sure I was out there, and it's none of your business where I've been, what I've done, or where

I'm going, Wheeler!"

Wheeler smiled, but his eyes never left Doc Jeff. "You sound kinda tough, vet. Be sensible, an' play your cards close to your chest, savvy? Forget that cow-man. Play along with me and my farmers . . ."

Something told Doc Jeff that this setup was phony. It was too staged, too patent. A coldness came across the vet's back and warned him of danger.

Wheeler had stopped him in an ideal spot . . . ideal for trouble. He got the impression that Wheeler wanted trouble, too. Wheeler was warning him to swing against the cowmen, especially the Endicott Quarter Circle U cow outfit.

Jeff thought, 'The dirty devil,' and he felt his temper rise.

"When I got out of college a few months ago, Wheeler, I took an oath to treat any sick animal, regardless of who owned that animal — be the owner a friend or an enemy. And mister, I intend to stick by that oath, come hell or high water, or both."

Wheeler smirked. "Sometimes an oath is just a waste of words. A lot of wind, vet."

"Mine wasn't," Jeff assured him.

Wheeler's heavy eyes rested on him. Despite his seemingly lazy posture in the saddle, Jeff got the impression that the land-locater was tough underneath, willing and ready to meet any trouble — with guns, fists, or just plain brute force.

Wheeler's eyes were sharp pinpoints against Doc Jeff. "Jones, you know I kinda like you, even with your stubbornness and lack of foresight. You'd be a good man to have on my side. I won't threaten you, because I got a hunch a threat won't do a bit of good."

"That's right, for once, Wheeler."

Wheeler showed a tight smile. "So, instead of threatenin' you, I'll appeal to your logic and intelligence. Endicott is only a rancher, and just *one* rancher, too. Savvy?"

"Keep talking. You're about as interesting as nothing, Wheeler."

"My talk will get more interestin' as I go on, vet. Endicott, like I said, is only one man, while I got about twenty farmers located on Scrub Pine land. Does that mean anything to you?"

"Keep talking."

"You can add, and you can read and write. That means the odds are twenty to one. Too big to gamble on, so why not be smart, vet, and sign up with my farmers against Endicott?"

Doc Jeff saw through the trap at this point. Everything suddenly shifted and gained lines of clarity. If he did not agree with Wheeler, he would be in for a mess of trouble. Wheeler might kill him. That thought was logical. You could kill a man here in this lava-bed country, carry his body off the trail, and throw him into a deep crevice.

Wheeler was ambitious. To gain success, he had to break the Endicott spread, and he, Doc Jeff, was helping Endicott — not directly helping to fight

Wheeler and his farmers, but indirectly so by attempting to save Endicott's cattle from blackleg.

This was, in a measure, ironic, and this irony showed on Doc Jeff Jones's boyish face. Wheeler was against him, wanted his blood; so, for that matter, did Endicott. He was caught in the middle.

"Were you out to doctor that sick bull, Jones?" Wheeler asked.

"How come you know that Endicott had a sick bull, Wheeler?"

Wheeler paused; for a moment, his face seemed to show something. Then he said smoothly, "Word got around that the Endicott kid came into town asking for you to doctor a bull suspected to have blackleg disease. But that ain't neither here nor there. I asked you a question, put a proposition up to you."

Suddenly both men stiffened. First, Doc Jeff Jones heard the roar of wings. The sound, coming so unexpectedly, startled him. Then his surprise subsided as he saw a big brush owl suddenly roar out of the lava rocks about a hundred feet away. The owl roared upward, wings clawing the air. Apparently he was in great haste to get away from his resting place. Usually, in the daytime, these owls never moved, for they could not see. Something — or somebody — had surely scared this big fellow.

Jeff knew, then, what had scared the owl. Unless he was plum wrong, Lee Osborne was crouched back there in the rocks, and Osborne had a gun on him. This caused fear to lance through the veterinarian. But his jaw was hard and set when he looked back at Wheeler.

"*Get out of my way!*"

"Make me move, cow doc!"

There the challenge lay bare — ugly, mean, sinister. Jeff controlled his temper, for temper had no place here. Had he been sensible, he would have played up to Wheeler, but that thought was repugnant.

If he did that, people would claim

24

he was one of Wheeler's men, and Millicent would not like that. Odd to think of Millicent at this moment! But it was now or never with Wheeler, even if Wheeler did have a gunman staked out in the rocks.

Jeff gritted, "I'll move you, Wheeler!"

Again Wheeler eyed him. He leaned forward in his saddle, his face closer. His smile was thin, and he was opening his mouth when Jeff's fist smashed in and caught him on the jaw.

Doc Jeff hit with hard swiftness. His only hope was to lay Wheeler cold, then pile off his bronc to the ground and fight Lee Osborne on foot.

Teeth gritted, he heard the hard click of Wheeler's molars smashing shut. Desperately, he hoped that his blow would smash Wheeler out of his saddle. But it did not completely knock the land-locater out of leather. Wheeler sagged and almost lost his stirrups. Jeff went out of his saddle, body lunging forward, using his stirrups for a springboard. His arms went out, and he tackled Wheeler around the belly with such hard and driving force that both he and Wheeler went to the ground.

But old Lady Luck once again frowned on Doc Jones. And, in frowning on Jeff, she smiled on Wheeler. For Wheeler, groggy and almost out on his feet, landed on top of Jeff.

With a sickening, crushing force, the ground reared up and hit Doc Jeff. He landed on a rock about the size of a cup, and it crashed into his back, almost paralyzing him. Wheeler, a heavy man, landed on top of him.

Wheeler snarled, "You cheap two-bit hoss doctor! Tried to kill me with one blow, eh?"

He spat in Doc Jones's face and smashed his big right fist, about the size of a small ham, into Jeff's nose and flattened it.

Stars exploded. Dazed, almost knocked unconscious, Jones fought by instinct. Instinct got his knees pounding upward — both knees, bony knees — and they hit Wheeler hard in the back, sending him forward with an agonized lurch.

Then Doc Jeff had both boots planted solidly against Wheeler's belly. He kicked and almost lifted Wheeler off the ground. He heard the land-locater gasp — an agonized sound. Wheeler went backward, arms flailing, and crashed into a boulder; his head lurched back and hit the lava rock with a loud crack. Already Jeff was on his feet, moving in, fists up. By now his head had cleared somewhat.

But Wheeler had no more fight. The slap of his head against the boulder had knocked him out. Jeff, remembering that Osborne was undoubtedly in the rocks, moved with flashing suddenness. Legs digging, he almost dived into the rocks for safety. He fell down and rolled over, expecting a bullet to hit him any moment. But no bullet came, and he hunkered under a boulder's overhang, his .45 in his hand.

Crouched there, breathing like a

wind-broken horse, many thoughts screamed through his mind. Chief of these was that Osborne would have a gun — either a short-gun or a rifle. And Osborne would be out to kill him.

Head canted, he listened. The silence that had suddenly settled — the thick and ponderous silence of the sunset — was finally broken by the sound of a horse stamping against the indignities of a pestering horsefly. The sound came from the rocks.

Doc Jeff decided to change positions. Logic told him that Osborne would work up higher on the ledge, for the man who had the altitude would win in this battle — if he were higher than his opponent, he could shoot down and kill him. It seemed odd that he, Doc Jeff Jones, the veterinarian, would want to kill a man. But Osborne, he reasoned, would be out to kill him. And he aimed to kill him first.

3

SO far, no shots had come from Osborne, which told Jeff that the gunman was not watching him. This was a cheering thought that did much to drive the pain out of his back as he worked upward, always upward, darting from boulder to boulder, his .45 gripped in his fist, his eyes missing nothing.

Then a shot rang out; it came from below him. Osborne had glimpsed him as he made a move to another boulder. Doc Jeff heard the sound of steel hitting lava rock, and instinctively he ducked. The bullet slammed itself into space with a screaming whine. By this time, Doc Jeff was among the rocks, safe from another shot. Then the report came in, moving through the dusk, a loud and terrible sound. This in turn died, and Doc Jeff was only aware of his hoarse, animal breathing.

He lifted his .45 and aimed at the spot from which the smoke and lead had come — a dip in the rocks below him. He could not see Osborne, for evidently the man was hidden back there — crouched, tough, watching.

Suddenly he screamed, the sound ringing across the rocks, losing itself in the thin air.

"You — got — me, Osborne. Don't shoot no more. I lost my gun."

Then, grinning like a bobcat that had just caught a sage hen, he hunkered in his hiding place and waited patiently.

"Where you at, Jones?"

Doc Jeff did not answer. He wanted to give the impression that he was unconscious. After a while, he became aware of a scuffling sound somewhere to his right. He frowned and considered its source. Osborne was at his left and below him. This sound had come from his right. He wondered if a cougar had been sunning himself in the lava rocks, became frightened, and slunk away, accidentally dislodging a rock as he sought safety deeper in the badlands.

"Where you at, Jones?" Again Osborne called the question. And again Doc Jones did not answer. His own nerves were getting raw. Possibly he had heard no cougar; in fact, maybe there had been no sound at all.

He felt faint and almost passed out. Doggedly, he shook his bloody head, fighting to remain conscious; again he thought he heard a strange sound. But he blamed it on the sudden breeze that had come out of nowhere to sing through the jagged boulders. The breeze felt good, though; it helped clear his head.

He decided to work down-slope, heading toward Osborne. He had to shoot down the man in a hurry, for soon Wheeler would come to and get in the fray. And he couldn't hope to fight both men and whip them. They would split up and converge on him, and even if he got one of them, the other would undoubtedly kill him.

He moved ahead, bent over. As he went around a rock, he spotted a sandy strip ahead of him about five feet wide and about fifty feet long, a strip of sand washed down by the rains.

Suddenly he stiffened. Somewhere beyond the big boulder at the far end of this strip he had heard the shuffle of boots and a man's voice saying, "Hey, what — "

And another voice had said, "Put your hands up and keep them up. I'll let this hammer fall if you don't raise your hands — That's good!"

A strange voice. The first speaker, Doc Jeff realized, had been Lee Osborne. But the second — ? He couldn't believe his ears.

The second voice said, "I got him, Jeff. Oh, Jeff, where are you?"

"Coming across the sand strip."

He hurried forward, for he knew now who owned that second voice. He reached the middle of the sand strip and stopped. His knees threatened to buckle, and the world swam. With difficulty, he got his vision cleared, his knees tough.

Around the corner of the far boulder came a man, hands high. Lee Osborne, his face twisted with rage, was not nice to look at. At first, Jeff could not see the person behind Osborne. Then, as they came closer, he saw he had correctly recognized the owner of the second voice. "Millicent!"

"Nobody else, Jeff. Came out to meet you, saw this ruckus from the ridge, and came down to help you. Slug this gent hard, and we get out of here pronto, or else Wheeler will come to and get into this mess."

"Logic," Jeff grunted.

He came close and Osborne attempted to duck. Jeff's .45 clipped the gunman and knocked him cold to the sand.

"That settles him," Millicent said shakily. "Now let's get broncs and hail out of here, Jeff."

Jeff grinned. "With pleasure."

They roared across the prairie, broncs running low to the ground. Doc Jones, glancing at Millicent, liked what he saw. The wind whipped her red hair back, for her Stetson, held by a strap, dangled behind her.

She turned her blue eyes on him and asked, "How do you feel, Jeff?"

"With my fingers."

"Quit trying to act like a schoolkid. How is the head?"

"When I look at you," Doc Jeff said, "my head goes around and around, and I'm on the merry-go round of love."

"Oh, shut up. Such nonsense."

They galloped along, horses running hard. Jeff hollered, "In all sincerity, honey, you sure saved this vet's hide. Those boys aimed to polish me off, or I'm sure mistaken."

Her face, usually laughing and gay, was very serious. "I came just as you and Wheeler had your fight. Luckily nobody saw me. I was lucky to get my rifle against Osborne's back, too."

Jeff said, "Honey, you took a terrible chance. He could have turned and killed you. Lord, just to think of it makes my blood cold. These two are really out for blood. It seems odd they would try to kill me just because I helped Endicott. That doesn't seem motivation enough for a murder, does it?"

"To them it does."

Jeff shook his head. "I still doubt that they aimed to kill me. They just figured they'd scare me into kingdom come with their guns and make me swear to work only for the farmers. Murder is a serious charge, Millicent."

"Not if it is never brought to light, Doc Jeff."

"I still think they just aimed to beat the daylights out of me and let it go at that." Gingerly, he touched his battered nose and his upper lip, which was now swollen. "And maybe they did just that. Heck, Millie, they got this boy caught in the middle of hell!"

"That's an understatement, Jeff!"

Jeff grinned crookedly. "Seems odd you'd come out to look for me, girl. Last night, big as life and prettier, you paraded down the aisle of that tent show perched on the big shot's arm. Now you switch your attentions from Mr. Big to a poor, beaten-up, lowdown veterinary. Women are hard to understand."

"You *were* talking sense," Millicent said, essaying seriousness. "Now you're just talking, Doc."

"Well, they got Doc Jeff Jones plumb in the middle, honey. If I doctor one of Endicott's Quarter Circle U critters, I'm helping the ranchers, and therefore I automatically become an enemy of the farmers."

"Looks that way."

"Then, if I doctor a farmer's critter, I'm automatically the friend of the farmers, and then I'm Endicott's enemy."

"You sure are caught on the horns, Doc Jeff."

He canted his head, apparently giving this predicament serious thought. But he had gone over it many times before and had already decided on a course of action. Nevertheless, he wanted to see what effect, if any, his next words would have on one Millicent Simmons.

"Well, I could leave the country for once and for always."

She glanced at him quickly. "Are you serious, Doc Jeff?"

"Sure I'm serious. These farmers and the ranchers are going to war — open and dirty warfare. Somebody will get killed. A bullet kills without a thought or a bit of remorse. And that bullet might kill me."

"You won't run."

"What makes you say that?"

"You're too stubborn to run. You got stubbornness written all over you — in your face, your eyes. Don't worry, you'll stay until the last dog is hung!"

"Mind reader besides being a good cook, eh?"

"I know something about men. I don't watch them shovel grub into their faces all day without learning something about them."

Jeff grinned, then grimaced. His

lips hurt. "Blackleg germs," he said. "Endicott's bull has blackleg."

"Are you sure?"

"I'm not wrong, Millicent."

She frowned prettily. The freckles across her nose made her even more attractive. "They say that blackleg has never been on Scrub Pine range before. So how would the germ suddenly get into cattle at this particular time?"

"A farmer might have brought in a cow that is a carrier of blackleg germs. That is possible. Some critters never get sick but just carry the disease, like some humans carry T.B. and apparently don't suffer themselves from the disease."

Again she frowned. "Tell me about blackleg. How does it start? What does it do to cattle? How do they get it, and how do you keep it from spreading in a herd, Doc Jeff?"

"You're asking for a semester's course in vet medicine, honey, but I'll do the best I can because *you are you* — despite my aching, throbbing head."

Their broncs had slowed to a walk. "First, blackleg was caused by bacteria, and this bacteria went under the high falutin' name of *clostridium chauvei*. Blackleg bacteria not only attacked young cattle but also sometimes hit hogs and sheep. Cattle immediately got a high fever, and the skin on the shoulders became swollen and black."

"After the disease hits, how long does the animal live, Doc Jeff?"

"About twenty-four hours. Maybe, in some cases, a little longer."

"Then if Endicott's bull had blackleg, he should soon be dead?"

Doc Jeff Jones did not answer that immediately. Mrs. Endicott would sneak out to the barn and secretly vaccinate the sick bull, and if she did this, the chances were good that he would live. And the woman dare not tell her husband of her actions. This was a secret between Mrs. Endicott and him. He could not let Millicent in on it, despite his desire to do so. He really was caught in the middle.

"Yes, by all tokens, the bull should soon die."

"Tell me more about blackleg."

He was glad she had taken the subject of conversation away from the Endicott bull.

"Oh, more about blackleg, eh? Well, you asked for it, and here it is — another semester's course in veterinary medicine."

Blackleg was also known as *black quarter*. Another common name for it was *symptomatic anthrax*. The former name was derived from the fact that the front quarter of a stricken animal was first affected by the bacteria.

"The front quarters get stiff, and finally the animal cannot walk."

Jeff, just to be ornery, used some scientific terms, spouting them out with the power of a geyser spouting water. Millicent, of course, did not understand them. Jeff watched her and saw irritation creep across her face, giving her character and strength.

"Jeff Jones, if you are trying to act

smart with all those big words, you might just as well stop right now. You're impressing nobody, not even yourself!"

"You sure can deflate a guy in a hurry, honey."

"And I'm not honey . . . to you, anyway!"

"Are you honey to Wheeler?"

"Oh, please! How is blackleg transmitted from cow to cow! You said some cows are carriers. Is that the only way it is transmitted?"

"That is a good question. A cow can transmit it to grass, where it can lie dormant for years. Cattle graze on the grass, get the bacteria into them, and the disease takes hold."

"Then it can really spread and wipe out a herd?"

"It sure can, and fast — unless the young stock is vaccinated."

"Have you any vaccine?"

He told her he had a few bottles he had taken with him from college. She reminded him to order more, and he smiled ruefully and said, "Yeah, I'll order some . . . but it might not be sent to me from the wholesale house."

"Why not?"

"You want me to turn my pockets inside out?"

"Are you that flat, Doc?"

"I haven't taken in much money. The farmers are poor and sometimes can't pay. I thought when I came I'd make some money off Endicott. But he's danged near ordered me off his ranch for good."

"Poor Doc Jones. Your credit is good at the Branding Iron Cafe, Doc. Millie won't let her doc go hungry."

"All joking aside, I might have to call you on that."

She smiled sweetly. "Maybe some farmer's wife will obligingly have a baby for you to deliver. They'll have to pay for the child, or else you keep him."

"Oh, Lord," Jeff groaned.

"Look, let's get on safer ground, eh? How do they make vaccine?"

"A patent process. You take matter from a vesicle and transfer it to glycerine solution. Then this solution is hermetically sealed for proper use at the proper time. Injection into the afflicted animal is made with a hypodermic needle. Is that clear?"

"About like mud. Talk English, not Chinese."

"All right, Teacher Jones will be patient with his not-so-bright pupil. Dead bacteria is taken from an afflicted animal. This is put into a solution of glycerine that is injected into a living animal. Almost like vaccination in a human, only a cow has thicker hide."

"Sometimes."

They rode down the alley behind her cafe. She was going to give him some headache powder. They dismounted, and he led her horse into the barn, leaving his mount in the alley.

"Where's the powder, Millie?"

"In my room, of course. Where do you think I keep it — out here in the garbage can?"

"Don't get cynical," he joked. "I wonder if it is safe for a handsome young man like me to be alone in the same room with a ruthless young woman like you. You promise I'll be safe?"

She pushed him through the door. "Sit in that chair, keep your mouth shut, and don't look at me that way. You look like a hungry pooch looking at a ham bone."

Jeff sat stiffly on the chair. She had gone into the kitchen, and he heard her turn on the tap. Scrub Pine had running water that came from a spring up on the hill beyond town.

The small house had another room, too. Through the open door of this room he could see the bottom part of a bed — a bright-blue bedspread. A thick rug covered the floor. The place was as immaculate as the head of a polished pin. The furniture was not new, but it was substantial.

"Sure different from my vet shop," he muttered.

She came back with a glass of water. "Here, drink this, and I'll be happy. It'll keep your mouth closed for a little while!"

Jeff almost gagged on the cream-colored liquid. Finally he got it down and handed the glass back to her.

"You sit here and rest a moment while I check in on my restaurant."

She went out the bedroom door. Then he heard her opening the back door of her cafe and talking to her cook. Something had evidently gone wrong during her absence. In no uncertain terms, she was laying down the law.

Jeff smiled. Millie had two sides. One was soft and feminine, the womanly, motherly side. The other, which she showed her customers and the world, was businesslike.

Jeff thought, I like her better as a woman!

Millicent looked in. "How do you feel?"

"Better, thanks."

"I'll be busy for a while with the

45

supper rush, but you can sit and rest as long as you like, Doc."

"I gotta be moving, kid."

"Take it easy. I'll bring you some supper."

She returned to her dining room. He heard the door close, and all was quiet except for the faint murmur of voices from the kitchen.

Doc Jeff stretched out his legs, decided the chair was too hard, and moved over to the Morris chair. He put his head back and shut his eyes. He thought of Matt Wheeler and Lee Osborne. Had they really wanted to kill him? Or had they just set out to scare him from doctoring any of Endicott's cattle in the future?

He knew that Wheeler and Osborne were settling dumb farmers on land totally unfit for farming. Wheeler and Osborne knew that, too. Then why did they have farmers squat on such poor land? Was it for the hundred-dollar filing fee?

This Scrub Pine land was only fit

for graze land. And not much good for that, either. It took about ten acres to support one cow. The land could be farmed, but would produce little; the soil was saturated with black alkali, which killed the seeds. Then, too, rain-fall was very scant — not more than about six or eight inches a year. High mountains penned in the range. The clouds dropped their moisture on these mountains either in the form of snow or rain, and by the time they reached the valley, they were devoid of moisture.

His mind went to the Endicott bull. If the bull died, Endicott would be forced to admit his diagnosis had been correct. But if the bull lived . . .

He sure was caught in the middle. He had wanted to be neutral. But Osborne and Wheeler had put the pressure on him, had tried to force him to side with the farmers. Every cow that Endicott lost made the side of the hoemen stronger. If blackleg got into Endicott's herds, it might break the Quarter Circle U. Which was what Wheeler and Osborne — and the farmers — wanted.

Doc Jeff sat up suddenly. From the kitchen had come the sound of a harsh and excited voice.

"Where is Doc Jones?"

Jeff was on his feet, for the voice belonged to Old Man Dial, a local oldster whom Jeff had been good to and had fed many times when he had only a few dimes in his pocket himself.

"He's out in my front room, Mr. Dial." That was Millicent Simmons's voice. "Is something wrong?"

"I gotta see Doc."

The old man barged into the room, a thin shadow in the dim dusk. His thin face, matted with whiskers, showed high excitement.

"Jeff, I jes' come from your office. They's a gent sneakin' around there. He didn't see me, I saw him."

"Who is he?"

The old man's voice was hoarse.

48

"He's that new gent what works for Matt Wheeler. Name of George Miller, I think."

Jeff remembered Miller — short, heavy, mean-looking.

He ran out the door, and the old man followed him.

4

DOC JEFF JONES had sprinted in college, but he had never traveled the hundred-yard dash any faster than he did when he ran up the alley toward his office. Thoughts clicked into place. It all hinged around his fight with Wheeler.

Miller evidently figured Wheeler and Osborne had downed him back there in the lava country. Now he intended to openly wreck the office-laboratory, under Wheeler's orders, of course.

Another thought hurried in, held its place, then was whisked away. All the blackleg vaccine around Scrub Pine was in that office. Not much, as he had told Millicent; still, if Miller smashed the vials, cattle would die like flies.

The back door of his office faced the alley. Jeff saw the dark form of a man crouched below the door knob, trying to fit a key to the lock. When the man heard him, he hurriedly jerked himself upright.

Jeff tackled him head on.

He had played end on the college football team, and he used all this experience now. His shoulder smashed against Miller's barrel chest with terrific force. The blow, crashing in, turned the man, driving him against the log wall. Doc Jeff heard his agonized grunt.

Miller had a bunch of keys in a ring. The keys flew one way; he went the other. Doc Jeff heard the sharp clang as the keys hit a rock in the alley. But he had no ears for the metallic sound. His hands were busy with George Miller.

Miller clawed for his .45, still in holster. Jeff, checking himself, glimpsed the movement and hit with savage hardness. He felt his fist smash into the corded muscles of Miller's belly.

Miller grunted, and his hand released his gun's grip. Quickly, Jeff had the .45; he threw it down the alley and it landed beside the ring of keys.

Miller grunted, "I'll beat the heck outa you — "

Miller knew all the dirty holds, all the dirty tricks. He was an expert at this rough-and-tumble fighting. Jeff realized, with grim certainty, that he had a fight on his hands, and he would be indeed lucky if he whipped this gunman. He had gone through one tough fist-fight. Now he was in another, maybe a tougher one.

He had to end it soon, or Miller would end him. His .45 flashed up, then came down. But Miller, quick as a cat, had turned, and the heavy barrel caught him across the shoulder, missing his ugly head.

"Jones, I'll kill you — "

Jeff raised the gun again, face savage in determination. Miller pivoted, a huge cat in Justin boots, and, without another word, he ran down the alley. Doc Jones, running grimly, brought him down with a hard flying tackle. He had never tackled a man that hard in his life, not even on the gridiron.

Miller's head popped back and, for a moment, Doc Jones saw the man's protruding, agonized eyes bulging in their sockets.

Then Jeff's grip was torn loose, and he rolled over. Miller rolled, too, but Miller had had enough. The buckle on his gunbelt broke, and the belt fell into the dust.

Miller got to his feet and ran like the devil was chasing him with a red-hot pitchfork. He skidded around a corner, dust lifting, and then he was gone from view. Doc Jeff sat in the alley, skinned and dirty, and had not the situation been of such grim nature, he would have laughed at Miller's hurried flight.

Old Man Dial roared, "You shore got him on the run, Doc! Man alive, wish somebody could have seen that. You tackled him so hard his eyes popped open. What a gunman!"

"He's tough enough," Doc Jeff panted. "He just never got a chance, that's all." He couldn't say anything more; he was puffing like a steam engine on a siding. Then he stooped and picked up the ring of keys and Miller's gun. He jammed the gun into his belt, and carrying the keys, went out on the main street, where a man said, "What happened to your face, Doc Jeff?"

"Looking for you, Deputy Coogan. George Miller tried to break into my office. Here are some keys he was using to try to open the door. Here's his .45, too. When you see him, give him these with my compliments."

The deputy was a short, stolid man who chewed tobacco eternally. If there had been a tax put on brain power, the people would have owed him money, or so Doc Jeff Jones figured. Now Deputy Sheriff Chuck Coogan chewed diligently, his fat face puckered into what was supposed to be a frown that denoted deep thinking, but which, in fact, looked rather comical.

"Done seen Miller run hell-for-leather down the alley for his bronc.

You say he was a-tryin' to break into your office, Doc?"

"That's what I said, Coogan."

Tobacco rolled, found a new spot, and began to be pounded between molars again. "Why for he want to break into your spread, Doc?"

"Wreck the outfit, of course. Break up my bottles of blackleg vaccine, I suppose."

The deputy peered at him. "No blackleg disease on this range, Doc."

"Heck of a lot you know about it," Doc Jones said. He was going to add some caustic remark, but held it back in time. There was no use needling this deputy. His brain power was limited. Besides, he had enough trouble at home, Doc Jeff had heard; Mrs. Coogan, so Millicent had said, had a tongue with a double-edged razor blade in it.

"I seen Miller try to break in," Old Man Dial told Coogan. "I was the one what ran fer to git Doc."

"You seen him try to fit the keys?"

"I sure did."

Coogan rolled his cud again. "If'n you got thet much evidence, you kin swear out a warrant for Miller, an' I'll serve it. But I still cain't see why he, almost a stranger here, would want to wreck Doc's outerfit."

They were walking down the alley. Doc Jeff Jones led the way, with Old Man Dial trailing, the deputy in the rear.

"Miller works for Wheeler," Doc Jones pointed out. "Wheeler wants me off this range unless I tend only to cattle that belong to the farmers. You ask me how come I got this lovely-looking face, Coogan. Well, I'll tell you."

Doc Jeff then told him about his fight in the lava-bed country. For once, Deputy Sheriff Chuck Coogan did not chew his tobacco. His mouth opened a little at first, then slowly shut itself, but his teeth did not pulverize his cud. "An' little Miss Millicent — she saved you, eh, Doc? Jus' last night Matt

56

Wheeler beaued her to the tent show, an' today she throws a gun against Lee Osborne, Wheeler's top man! Wheeler won't like that."

"To blazes with what he likes," Doc Jeff growled, putting his key in the lock.

"He's got a lot of influence."

Doc Jeff grunted, "I'm not in a political job like you are. To heck with him and his influence — if he has any."

"Miller got so scared he done left town," the deputy chuckled. "No complaints to be filed then, eh, Doc?"

"None."

The deputy turned and left, boots moving down the alley. And Doc Jeff glanced at Old Man Dial when the oldster said thoughtfully, "Never could figger out whether thet deputy was jus' plain all-fired lazy or just too dumb to count."

"He can count his dollars each payday," Doc Jeff said. "Thanks for watching over my outfit, Old Man.

Here's a buck for your trouble."

"I'd do it fer free, Doc, fer you."

Still, the old man took the dollar. Doc Jones was hoping the recluse would turn down the offer, for he needed that dollar for himself. But it went into the deep pocket of the old man's torn pants.

"Seems odd Miller would run out of town like that," the old man mused. "Well, got a couple widows I gotta attend to, Doc."

That was an old and threadworn joke. Old Man Dial was always in love with some young widow — according to him.

Jeff went inside his office. Suddenly, it struck him odd, too, that Miller would leave. From the sounds made by his bronc's hoofs, one would figure he had headed toward the lava beds. Had he gone out there to meet Matt Wheeler and Lee Osborne? By all rights, the pair should have been in Scrub Pine by now; that is, if they had ridden toward town after the fight. Maybe they hadn't returned to Scrub Pine. Maybe they had headed out to visit and talk with some of the farmers, or maybe they had drifted out to Wheeler's homestead to growl and snarl and lick their wounds.

Jeff lit a lamp and, in its feeble rays, inspected his face in the mirror. He got the iodine bottle and applied a drop here and there to cuts and scratches. This done, he went out, locking the door. On the way to the cafe, he had to walk past Matt Wheeler's office, a log building on Sagebrush Avenue, Scrub Pine's main street.

The office had a good-sized front window, and on it, painted in high letters, was the sign:

Matt Wheeler
Land-Locater   Land Agent
Farmers, See me first!
I save you money!

What a lie, Doc Jeff thought.
The deputy came out of the shadows.

"Wheeler ain't home yet, Doc Jeff. I'm lopsided from carryin' Miller's gun around. You took it from him. Why don't you give it an' the keys back to Miller?"

"You scared of him?"

"I don't care to muscle in on trouble, Doc Jeff."

Jones had a sudden thought that prompted a crooked smile. "All right, Coogan, I'll give them to him or Wheeler."

"Good."

The deputy turned and went into a saloon. For a moment, Doc Jeff stood and smiled, and his eyes, even in the semi-darkness, held a wicked glow. He returned to Wheeler's office, and again he studied the big glass window. Then he looked covertly up and down Sagebrush Avenue.

Old Man Dial was the only one on the street; he ducked into the saloon, and Doc Jeff thought, "There goes my hard-earned buck for whiskey."

The door closed behind Old Man

Dial. The street was without occupants, and no eyes save his own saw Doc Jeff Jones throw the six-shooter and the keys through the window of Matt Wheeler's office. The glass went in with a loud crash.

Deputy Coogan charged out of the saloon, beer bottle in hand. "What the heck broke out here, Doc Jeff? Sounded like glass — "

"I went to hang that gunbelt and gun on the door, but somehow the gun swung around and hit the window and broke it. They sure make poor glass nowadays. Look how that thing busted — a million pieces — and all an accident."

"You cut yourself, Doc?"

"A little bit, on my hand." He showed the deputy the cut. The deputy did not, of course, know the cut had come from a jagged rock during the lava-bed fight with Matt Wheeler.

Deputy Sheriff Coogan's eyes bugged. "Well, I'll be hanged, but you did. Sure was a poor piece of glass. Wheeler sure will belch fire when he sees it busted!"

Old Man Dial held a whiskey bottle. "Let him get mad," he said philosophically. "This ain't no kentry to get these dumb farmers into to starve to death. Somebody oughta make Wheeler quit them monkeyshines."

"What do you know about it, you ol' stiff?" a farmer demanded. "You only know which end of a hoss gets the crouper. You don't know a disc from a harrow."

"That's right, farmer. And what's more, I have no intention of knowin' the difference. I aim to stay in total igguerance."

"Let's head inside," another man said. "No excitement out here."

That left Doc Jeff and Deputy Coogan alone. And the deputy said, "Sure an odd accident, Doc." He wouldn't come right out and say Doc Jeff had deliberately broken the window, although it was plain he was suspicious.

"Too bad, Deputy. But I sure won't pay for it."

"Should've hung on to that artillery myself and this would never have happened. Wheeler will sure boil over — "

Doc Jeff, grinning widely, was moving toward the Branding Iron Cafe, leaving Deputy Coogan to contemplate the wrath of one Matt Wheeler, a bogus land-locater. He went into the cafe, spun a stool, and slid onto it. He was the only customer in the place.

Millie came out of the kitchen, face flushed from the heat of the stove. He looked at her and liked what he saw: a bright print dress, a white starched apron, and a neat little band around her red hair. Yes, and the freckles, too.

"Heard you broke a window in Wheeler's office."

"I didn't break *a* window, I broke *the* window." He added hastily, "All an accident, of course. I was deliverin' some of Miller's articles, and Miller's

63

gun swung around and it hit the glass — and that's it, Millicent."

"An accident, eh?"

"Don't you believe me?"

"No, I don't. And you had another fight, too, Old Man Dial told me. You knocked George Miller galley west. What did he aim to do if he had got into your office?"

"Destroy the blackleg vaccine, I think."

Her eyes narrowed. "That would be a terrible thing to do, Jeff. That would leave innocent cattle to die, to suffer from blackleg. But you can't prove that, though."

"No, I can't. No more than Wheeler can prove I deliberately broke his window."

"Breaking that window settled nothing."

"I know that. But it gave me lots of satisfaction."

She wiped the bar with a towel. Over the entire range hung the dark and terrible cloud of danger. Endicott

64

ran cattle over land he claimed by squatter's rights and not by filed deeds. He looked upon this range as his private kingdom. He had fought the redskins for it, and he had helped eradicate the shaggy buffalo so that his longhorns could graze. Now a tamer group was taking this land from him. Endicott and his riders would fight, and men would die.

"This whole town, this whole range — It's jittery, Doc Jeff."

Doc Jeff picked up a menu. He could see his face in the bar mirror. He was not a romantic-looking young veterinarian. His face looked as if it had been run over by a wagon wheel. His right eye was getting a definite bluish-black tinge.

"I'll take a beefsteak."

"I have your supper on the back of the stove. You barged out of my house so fast, I didn't have time to feed you. And you'll not have beefsteak unless you want to use it on your eye."

"What you got cooked for me?"

65

"Ham, sir, ham."

"You sit by me and hold my hand. Tell the cook to bring out the victuals."

"The cook is here no more, kind sir. He had a bottle cached out. He got drunk. I fired him. I am cook, hasher, and bottle-washer in this dive. You eat what I serve and pretend to like it."

"You'd be a hard woman on a loving husband."

"You are not my husband, thank God!"

"I might be someday."

"I doubt that."

Doc Jeff suddenly decided to close his big mouth. Husbands supported families, and families demanded money, and he had no money — only hopes of a future. He decided to change the subject.

"Wheeler and Osborne aren't in town yet, eh?"

She slid onto a stool beside him. "Maybe Osborne had to take Wheeler over to the county seat to see the doctor. Your slugging fists did a little damage to his not-too-pretty features, or so it looked to me from a distance."

"Bet his head ached, too. He tried to dent that boulder with his head."

Millie watched him eat. "I don't quite understand this blackleg deal, Doc Jeff. Your diagnosis must be wrong."

"Why?"

"Well, what if somebody deliberately put a diseased animal on Endicott's range? Endicott would lose hundreds and hundreds of head of cattle, true?"

"That's right, unless he let me vaccinate his young stuff, which would call for another roundup."

She frowned prettily. "But the farmers would lose stock, too."

"They might let me vaccinate their stock."

"So would Mike Endicott, after his cattle really started dying. He's stubborn, but he'd never let his pride stand in front of his pocketbook, and each cow to him is so many bucks on the hoof."

"But his cattle would die like flies

before he would unbend that stupid cowman pride of his, Millie."

"The farmers would win a point there," she had to admit. "I hope your diagnosis on that bull is wrong."

"I do, too."

He was mopping up the last bite of ham when two riders rode past the cafe, the light shining on them.

"Wheeler and Osborne," Millie said.

Jeff paid, then said, "See you tomorrow, honey."

"Be careful — "

"I mean nothing to you. Remember, you told me that."

"Do you always joke?"

"Not when I sleep. Then I snore."

He went outside, feeling somewhat better. That had been a good meal! The way to his office took him past Matt Wheeler. Wheeler and Lee Osborne were inside, looking at the broken window. Wheeler held Miller's pistol and the keys.

Jeff stopped on the sidewalk, and they looked at each other, the broken window between them.

"It was an accident," Jeff said. "Miller got caught trying to unlock my office. I ran him out of town. Then I went to deliver his gun and the keys to you, and the gun swung around and accidentally broke the window."

Matt Wheeler glared at him. "Miller? What about him?"

"You should know," Doc Jeff Jones said. "You sicced him on me. He said that himself."

"He said no such thing."

"He might've told you different." Doc Jones did a little fabricating himself. "Anyway, he left town in a hurry, forgetting his gun and those keys." He looked at the gunbelt. "The buckle busted on that, and he lost it in the alley."

Deputy Sheriff Coogan, puffing like a wind-broken bronc, came charging in with, "No trouble here, you three."

Doc Jeff said, "You'll get no disturbance out of me, Deputy. I'm a tired man. Two fights in one day."

"Take it easy, Deputy," Matt Wheeler growled.

Doc Jeff looked at Lee Osborne. The gunman had his legs spread wide, hands on his two .45's, and he looked like anything but a hired farmhand, the alibi under which he traveled on this range.

Their eyes met. Osborne's held anger — bitter, driving anger. His lips curled, and he almost said something. Then discretion took over, closed his mouth, and made his eyes blank and unreadable.

Doc Jeff Jones looked at Matt Wheeler. Wheeler's eyes, hidden by swollen flesh, were ugly and mean, little pinpoints of hatred appraising him.

Jeff Jones smiled. He had won two fights, and yet he had lost. When he had fought Wheeler and Miller, he had, by his actions, brought himself down to their low estate, and he had lost some of his professional prestige. He turned and went to his office.

5

AFTER Doc Jones had ridden away from the Quarter Circle U corral, cowman Mike Endicott scowled and thought, '*That young vet might be right, at that.*' But he did not voice this to the hired hand. To him, he said, "We'll put this bull in a stall in the barn and watch him for a few days."

"You sure don't believe that hoss doc, do you, boss?"

"Not one bit, Jim."

They finally got the bull into the barn and tied in a stall. Mike Endicott mopped his forehead with a blue bandanna. "I'm gonna take a ride through the pasture where that bull was grazin', Jim. I'm gonna scout around. Why not saddle a bronc an' come with me?"

Although the ranch-owner had put

the request into a question, it was still an order; he seldom, if ever, directly ordered a man to do anything.

"Sure thing, Mike."

Within a few minutes, they were riding away from the ranch house, through the high cottonwood trees that grew along Doggone Creek, following the wagon road that eventually led to Scrub Pine. From the kitchen window, Clara Endicott watched them go out of sight. Now she hurried to the barn, her chickens following her, for it was close to their feeding time. The vaccine bottle and syringe had been hidden in the hay in a manger, and she was digging for it when her youngest son, Ray, entered the barn.

"Whatcha doin', Ma?"

"You run up to the house, young man. I'm looking for eggs."

"Bent over like that, diggin' in the hay? Hens don't bury their eggs, Ma."

She straightened, exasperated, glared at him. But he was not watching his mother. His boyish eyes were riveted

72

on something lying in the bottom of the manger, something glistening — the hypodermic needle.

"Ma, what is that thing?"

"Oh, heavens, I might just as well confess. If I don't, you'll run and blab to your father."

His mouth opened as she outlined her plan. His eyes glistened, too.

"I'll help you, Ma."

"But we both have to keep our mouths closed, Ray."

"I'll keep the secret till I die. Let's vaccinate this critter so fast he don't feel no pain." He studied the bull, and his fingers ran along the animal's shoulder. "His skin is crackly, Ma. Jus' like Doc Jeff said."

"Oh, merciful heavens."

The bull stood silently, suffering from the branding and the other indignities he had sustained at the cruel hand of man. Her fingers explored his shoulder, and both heard the crackling sound.

"Doc must be right," she said.

While he held the vaccine bottle, she

inserted the sharp needle through the seal. The needle went into the dark vaccine. Then she pulled back the plunger slowly, sucking the vaccine into the cylinder.

Ray squinted at the graduated scale on the glass wall.

"That's enough for one dose, Ma. Says so here on the bottle. Shucks, that's only blood! Will that stuff really save the bull from blackleg?"

"Doc says it will. Here, you hold the bull's skin, like that."

The bull did not object. When Ray grabbed the skin and held it in a bunched manner, Clara Endicott, the hypodermic syringe in hand, gritted her teeth.

"This is going to hurt me," she said.

"Not like it will hurt the bull."

"Here goes, Son."

Hurriedly, she ran the sharp needle through the thick hide. She remembered that Doc Jeff had said to insert the needle at a slant. This way, the tip would lie between the flesh and the hide.

The bull grunted moved a step, then stood still, the first shock of pain gone. Ray peered at the syringe, now sticking in the bull's shoulder.

"Looks all right to me. Now push down on the handle."

She pushed. Under pressure, vaccine left the cylinder. She slowly injected the vaccine into the body of the bull, then pulled the needle out; for some reason, she felt a little shaky at the knees.

Ray said, "We'll hide this outfit again. I know a better place than this manger."

"Hide it in the manger again."

Ray dug in the loose hay and dust and hid the syringe and the bottle. Then he looked at his mother. The significance of their act became greater with the passage of time.

"Dad hear about this, he'll bust his cinch."

"We won't tell him."

"He'd beat me," Ray said, "and

run you off Quarter Circle U range. Dad gum it, but I sure hope they ain't nobody killed when we tangle with them farmers, like Dad says we gotta do."

"Hush now with that talk."

"Well, Dad says — "

"Feed the bull some hay and forget what Dad says. Things will work out all right. They always do."

She returned to her empire, the kitchen. She wondered where her husband and Jim had ridden. She was, as usual, a little worried. Mike Endicott, she well knew, had a bad temper. Jim, though, was pretty levelheaded. They had probably ridden out to look over the range on South Fork. Mike had said the grass was getting short over there.

Her husband and Jim *had* ridden over to South Fork. And, while there, they had a run-in with Wheeler and Osborne.

Mike Endicott was in an angry mood. His trouble with Doc Jones did not sit well with him, and the sight of the new fences strung by the farmers added insult to injury.

"Hold in, Jim."

They were on a hill. Below them, barbed wire glistened, a silent challenge to their progress.

"New fence, boss."

"Another to rip out sometime." Mike Endicott swung his gaze across this range land, and then his anger increased. "Ain't that a new nester shack over yonder, Jim?"

Jim said, "Sure is. Wasn't there two days ago when I rode this country."

"Another poor critter shipped in by Wheeler to starve to death," Mike Endicott growled. "Darned fool, settled right in that bed of white alkali, too. All he can raise there is alkali weeds. That, and a fight, and we'll furnish the fight."

"Wheeler sure don't know land, boss."

Mike Endicott squinted at the shack. "Wheeler knows better'n that, Jim. He just wants their money. And the poor devils give him their last cent, too. Mind that farmer thet settled on Wolf Crick?"

"That tall one? Sure, I remember him. What about him?"

"He done left the country the other day. Had his bellyful of homesteadin'. He done sold his land to Matt Wheeler, they tell me."

"Wheeler bought his land?"

"Paid him thirty bucks for it. Quarter section. One hundred and sixty acres of no-good land ... only good for grazing. The nester couldn't raise a crop. Now, why would Matt Wheeler want the title to that no-good hunk of gumbo?"

Jim shrugged. "You got me, Mike."

Endicott spoke softly. "Maybe Wheeler's usin' them farmers. They get their deeds, starve out, then sell deeds to him. He gets patented land, and he runs cattle. And he's competition to us, mebbe no?"

"Could be, boss."

Endicott now had swung his field

glasses toward the western foothills. Here the hills reached their claws into the valley, rising slowly to meet the tumbled grandeur of the Rocky Mountains. But Endicott was not awed by the solemn lift of the mountains. About a mile away, two riders rode along the toes of the foothills, on a range claimed by the Quarter Circle U outfit.

Endicott said in a low voice, "Two riders over there, Jim."

Jim could scarcely see the riders, they were so far away. So he watched Endicott. And he saw Endicott's jaw go shut, his jaw muscles tightening.

Endicott lowered his glasses and handed them to Jim. "You look and tell me if I'm correct."

Jim focused the glasses on the two riders.

Mike Endicott said, "One is Lee Osborne, the two-bit gunslinger. An' the other is my bosom friend, nobody but Matt Wheeler."

"That's — right, boss."

"On our grass," Endicott said.

Jim said, "Sure as shootin'. And yonder is South Fork Crick, where that sick bull come from. That grass never had blackleg germs afore, boss."

"Ain't got it now!" Endicott was very curt.

Jim said nothing, but he watched the pair, mere dots against the endless sweep of this Montana range.

"Come on, Jim."

"Mike — "

"Come on!"

Already Mike Endicott was loping toward the pair, so Jim followed, dust lifting behind him. The encroaching pair saw them and drew in their broncs. They waited, watching them approach.

Wheeler said, "Endicott and that puncher called Jim. No trouble from us, Osborne!"

Lee Osborne's brows drew down sharply, bunching his heavy eyebrows. "All right, Matt," he said tonelessly. He added, "Unless they start trouble . . . "

Wheeler raised his right hand shoulder

high, palm out: the Sioux Indian sign of peace, an almost universal sign.

Lee Osborne crossed his arms on the fork of his saddle, leaning forward with hard and speculative eyes. With his arms crossed, both hands were close to his guns. All he had to do was straighten and come up with a cross-armed draw, a blazing gun in each fist.

Endicott and Jim drew rein, fussing up the dust a little. Then they sat there — four men appraising each other. And the dust settled slowly.

Finally Endicott broke the silence. "Why do you ride on my grass?"

Osborne said nothing, hands still over his guns. Jim watched Osborne and read him for a killer. And fear tugged at the cowpuncher. He was no gunman. Still, he watched Osborne. The air was tense. Then Wheeler brought his palm down. His shoulders lifted and fell, and his voice was lazy.

"Your grass, Endicott? How come it's your grass?"

"Squatter's rights, land-locater. Prior grazing rights."

Wheeler studied him; their gazes met and held. Both eyes held flint, but Endicott, not being subtle, showed his anger the more. Wheeler's anger was more submerged; only occasionally did it flare to the surface.

Endicott saw the man's swollen and beaten face. What had happened to Wheeler? Somebody had evidently worked him over with his fists.

"My grass," the cowman repeated.

"Squatter's rights and prior grazing rights do not hold in court."

"This won't get to court," Endicott said meaningfully. "The Quarter Circle U will see to that. Now, what are you doing on my grass?"

Wheeler spoke with determined solidness. "We heard you folks had a sick critter that had gazed on this grass, and we're looking over the rest of Quarter Circle U cattle to see if they got blackleg, too."

"There's no blackleg here. What

would it mean to you if there was blackleg on this grass?"

"My farmers. I have to protect my farmers."

Endicott snorted in derision. "Your *farmers*, eh? Your *suckers*, you mean!"

This was leading in only one direction — toward trouble. The words were pyramiding higher and higher, and another word or so would send them for their guns. Matt Wheeler, being a diplomat, withdrew. And through the land-locater's subtle withdrawal, Mike Endicott glimpsed the man's intelligence. Wheeler was patient. He would bide his time; he would sit and work, and he would watch. Patience, then, was a strong facet of his character; Endicott read this and saw that Wheeler owned what he lacked.

The land-locater said, "All right, cowman, We'll ride off what you call *your* grass." He looked at his gunman. "Come on, Lee."

"As you say, Matt."

They turned their broncs and loped

off in the direction of Scrub Pine. Mike Endicott and Jim sat their saddles and watched distance claim the pair.

Jim said, "They had somethin' more than their arms up their sleeves, Mike. They rode for some purpose, not just to look at our cattle."

"What would that purpose be?"

Jim drew long and deep of his Bull Durham, then regarded the cigarette and said, "You've got me stumped, boss."

Endicott flung out his right arm. "You ride to the north. I'll work the foothills."

"All right."

"You see any sick critters, haze 'em toward the home corral, Jim."

Endicott turned his mount, making him lope toward the brown hills. And as the horse traveled, Endicott thought: *'Wheeler had pulled in his horns fast, too fast. He had ridden away from trouble. And who had smashed in Wheeler's ugly face?'*

He rode through scattered bunches

of Quarter Circle U cattle, and the pride of possession was in him. These cattle — steers and cows and calves — grazed along the sides of hills, and fed in draws and coulees, for here grass was higher. Winter snows had stayed in low spots longer, thereby letting more moisture seep into the Montana earth.

He looked at his cattle, and the sight was good. For they were of strong blood, mostly Hereford strain. He had shipped in registered Hereford bulls to breed up his stock, and these bulls, crossed with native cows, had produced strong steers and heifers that could stand the torture of long, cold winters and could also endure the strong heat of midsummer. They were heavy with beef; they were tough.

One young heifer — a short yearling — limped slightly on its off-front leg. Endicott, remembering the sick bull, untied his lasso, hands trembling against the fork of his saddle. The loop came out, and he tied hard and fast, the twine tight around the saddlehorn. He rode close to the heifer. Did she have blackleg?

The heifer turned to run, and he rode in close, his lasso singing in short, angry hisses. The heifer lengthened, tail upraised, and the loop went ahead of her; for a moment, the noose lay on the soil, spread out and waiting for the heifer's forefeet, which quickly entered the snare, but not too fast for the cowman to jerk in the loop pulling it up around both front legs.

"Steady, hoss."

The horse, trained for this job, settled down on its haunches, forelegs stiff in the dust to better bear the shock as the heifer hit the end of the lasso. One moment the heifer was running level, tail raised, mouth open; the next, it was going tail over head, landing on its back with a startling force.

"Hold 'er, hoss!" Hogging string held between his teeth, the rancher hurriedly moved down the taut rope, coming in from behind the heifer. He pulled one hind leg close to its forelegs, his hands making fast movements with the hogging string. The heifer in the grass lay, kicking its free hind leg, unable to climb to its feet.

Endicott tugged on the catch-rope, and the horse moved ahead, giving him slack enough to disengage the rope.

The heifer lay on its side, eyes protruding and rolling with fear. Endicott's rugged fingers pushed along its shoulder, and he listened for the deadly crackle that bespoke of blackleg. But the skin, protected by the matted red hair, was cream-colored and clear, the shoulder not swollen. No blackleg.

Relief flooded the cowman. He looked at the heifer's hoof. There, jammed hard between the cloven hoof, was a round pebble.

He dug, got out his jackknife, and with the leather-punch blade, got the rock free. He went to his saddlebag and got a small bottle of turpentine and poured some over the injury.

Dusk was tiptoeing in, cooling the

world. He coiled his rope after turning the heifer loose, tied the lasso to his saddle, and went into leather with practiced ease.

Jim said, "Any sign of blackleg, boss?"

"Not a sign, Jim."

Jim sighed and said, "Good news." He showed a roguish smile. "Saw a Heart Nine rider over in the rough country about a hour ago. He'd been in town, and he told me some news."

"Yeah?"

"You know who beat the daylights outa Wheeler?"

"Who?"

"Doc Jones."

Mike Endicott studied his rider. "You really mean that, Jim?"

"So this rider told me. Doc an' Wheeler fought back in the badlands, right after Doc left our place this afternoon."

"He must have whupped Lee Osborne, too. The man that whups Matt Wheeler has to take on Osborne, or else I'm plumb wrong. Osborne had no fist marks."

"That's because of Millie Simmons, boss."

"Explain yourself."

"Well, Millie had rid out to meet Doc, and she saw Osborne hidin' in the lava rocks, so she sneaked down an' threw a gun on him."

"Well, I'll be hung an' rope cut!" Mike Endicott exclaimed.

6

HANDS on his holstered guns, Lee Osborne stood wide-legged in the office, watching Doc Jeff Jones cross Scrub Pine's main street. Occasionally, lamplight streaming from houses and stores along the street threw yellow light across the young vet, who apparently was going to his office.

Osborne said, "A couple of shots, boss, and he'd go down. And who would ever be able to pin his murder on me? Standing here in the dark, hidden from all eyes!"

"No gunplay, you fool."

"He's in the open — I could git rid of him."

"No gunplay, you hear me!"

Osborne turned on his heel, hands still anchored to his .45's. His voice was rigid and solid as he asked, "Why not?"

Wheeler sat in his swivel chair, looking at his broken front window. Anger seethed in him, but he kept this from his face.

"Light a lamp," he said.

Osborne crossed the room, glass grating under his boots. He found a match; his rough hands cupped it, and then the wick had fire. He replaced the chimney with, "Why don't you let me get him?"

"You shoot him down, and the whole range will know who did it, what with that trouble we've had with him today. We got to keep in the background, and not fight in the open, and you know darned well why, too!"

Osborne pulled back his hands from his gun-grips. "Yeah, we'd best walk on light boots, 'cause if we attract attention, word might come up from Arizona Territory about that Big Pine deal — "

"For Gawd's sake, shut your big mouth, Osborne!"

"Nobody can hear me but you."

"You don't know. So keep your mouth closed. George Miller thought nobody was watching him when he tried to open the door to Doc's lab'r'tory. But Old Man Dial seen him. You never can know for sure, Osborne."

"They say George Miller left the country."

Lamplight showed Matt Wheeler's grin. Then his gaze fell again on the shattered window, and that grin died.

"Miller's out at the cabin right now, waiting for us."

"He's a fool," Osborne growled. "Got a little drunk, and instead of trying to sneak into Doc's office, he openly tries to unlock it with some keys. A complete fool, that Miller."

Out of the space between the General Store and the blacksmith shop moved a dim, shadowy figure that became recognizable as it neared the lights of the store.

"Old Man Dial," Osborne breathed.

Matt Wheeler said, "An ol' gossip, provin' all gossipin' isn't done by women. He's the boy that tipped off Miller to the doc, they tell me."

Lee Osborne wet his thick lips and smiled. "He's a-headin' for his cabin along the crick, Matt. I could slip out the back, jump him down in the brush, and work him over with my pistol. And it would happen so fast in the dark he'd never know who did it. He'd think twice afore squealin' on us again."

Matt Wheeler shook his head.

"Why not, Matt?"

Wheeler looked at his gunman. "Use what little brains you got, Lee. We've run into a number of reverses today, so let's not make any more errors. Everybody has opened his big mouth and put his foot in it. Look at that fool of a Miller and the way he talked."

"He should have kept his mouth buttoned down, boss."

"Sure he should've. He should've never mentioned to nobody he was on our payroll. But he blows off his big mouth, and now everybody knows for sure we sicced him on Doc Jones. Now you aim to beat the daylights out of the old man." He shook his head sadly. "You fool! Do you think, for one minute, nobody'd know who worked Old Man Dial over?"

"They'd say you or me did it because he stooled on Miller."

"Man, what brain power!"

"I don't like this runnin' all the time, Wheeler."

Wheeler watched him. "When did we run?"

"From Endicott and this cowpuncher."

"What's wrong with that?"

"We're gonna get reputations of bein' cowards, Matt."

"That's all right. We sure don't want reps as gunfighters. We want to put over the impression to these saps that we're peaceful men and that we're trying to bring about peace between Endicott and the farmers. Our farmers, remember?"

"Then why did we jump Doc today out in the lava beds?"

"Nobody, normally, would have seen us work Doc over, and if he went to sign a warrant, it would have been our word against his — two against one. But then that heifer had to come in with her rifle — Man, this *has* been a bad day, eh?"

"We should've killed Endicott. That cowpoke he had with him was no gunslinger. I could have downed them both, and we could have hollered it was a fair fight, that Endicott pulled first. Everybody knows he has a rough temper."

Again Matt Wheeler shook his head. "We don't kill Endicott, savvy? Endicott will prob'ly get killed before this is over, but neither of us will kill him. One of our farmers might kill him, but not us."

"Our farmers," Osborne scoffed.

Wheeler made a steeple out of his two hands. He moved his thumbs and seemed interested in the movements. His voice was very low and very dry.

"Always remember we have to have

the farmers riled up against Endicott and that a little germ — a blackleg germ — is our friend. We have to break these farmers, put them on the rocks — "

Osborne paced to the window and pulled down the blind. He walked back and forth, boots grinding the glass occasionally and making a sharp noise hard on the nerves.

"That darn vet had to come along with his serum — "

"We have to make Endicott believe one of the farmer's cows brought in blackleg germs. We have to keep Doc Jeff from giving serum to the cows that get sick."

"Miller tried to get that serum. He failed."

"We'll get it. And what's more, we'll keep vaccine from getting into this basin. We'll wipe out the farmers and Endicott with blackleg, and then we'll own this grass. We'll rule the roost."

"What's next, Matt?"

"Night ride."

"Heck, we jus' got into town!"

"We head out again."

They went out the back door, walked down the alley, and approached a log barn on the edge of Scrub Pine. When they had ridden into town, they had racked their horses in the town livery. Now, if a person were to check on their broncs, they would see them in the town livery barn; therefore, the impression would be that the two were in town, probably asleep. Which was the way Wheeler wanted it.

They saddled in darkness and rode into the night. Nobody saw them leave Scrub Pine. Wheeler sought the lead, riding his stirrups, body angling forward. Osborne's horse pounded along, his head even with the flank of Wheeler's mount as they rode north. They finally forded a small creek, then rode through high brush, following a trail neither could see in the dark. Brush slapped against boots and leather chaps. They came to a small clearing, and here the night was not so dark. They could make out the small cabin sitting in that clearing — an outline in the darkness.

They drew rein in front of the cabin. Wheeler called, "Who's inside?"

No answer. Silence.

Wheeler knew a moment of bleak impatience as he repeated, "Who's inside? Miller, you in there?"

A man came out of the cabin. "That you, Matt?"

Both Wheeler and Osborne dismounted. Wheeler snarled, "Who do you figure it would be but me an Lee? What went wrong with you down in town, Miller?"

"Too many drinks, Wheeler."

Wheeler snarled, "After this, lay off the redeye. Doc sure trimmed your sails, fella, and you told me you were a gunman, a real gunslinger — "

"I'll make that vet fellow pay."

"Where is your bronc?" Wheeler asked.

"In the brush."

"Bring out the kerosene I told you to get?"

"On my saddle."

"Get your cayuse. We do some riding again."

Miller ran into the buckbrush. Wheeler lifted his bulk into the saddle; Osborne did the same. They curbed broncs, waiting. Miller rode back and said, "Five gallons of it. The cap leaks a little. I hate the smell of the stuff."

"You won't have to smell it very long."

"You stole the can at the Endicott spread?" Osborne asked.

"Sneaked in and got it from the tool shed. It's even got Endicott's Quarter Circle U iron painted on it in red letters."

"Good," Wheeler said.

Osborne grunted, "One thing that turned out right this day. Just one, though. The farmers'll blame this on Endicott."

"They'll be mad," Miller affirmed.

"Do you blame them?" Wheeler grinned. "A farmer's spread burns down. Then a five-gallon can that had kerosene in it is found. And painted on the can is the Quarter Circle U."

"An old trick," Osborne murmured.

Miller reined his mount close. "I waited a long time at the cabin, boss. Figgered you two would head in sooner. Somethin' hold you up?"

"We were out scouting and tangled with Endicott. He ordered us off his grass. But we learned what we wanted to learn."

They headed out, three men drifting under cover of black night.

"What did you learn?" Miller asked.

Wheeler said, "Endicott looked over that new shack the new farmer built in the middle of that worthless alkali bed. Endicott got mad when he saw that new shack."

"Yeah, an' then what?"

"Tonight that shack gets burned down."

7

SLOWLY, the sound penetrated the dark blanket of sleep that encircled Doc Jones. Somebody was knocking loudly at his door, and mingled with it was a man's shrill voice.

"Doc! Doc Jones!"

Doc Jeff sat up, sleep still clinging to him. "Who's there?"

"Terry. Terry Brendan!"

Brendan was the farmer who had built out on Wild Horse Flat, near South Fork. He had been on his homestead almost two months.

"What do you want?"

"My heifer — she's sick, Doc. I'm afraid she's gonna die — I want you to ride out and doctor her."

Doc Jeff thought, 'Another charity case.' "In the morning, Brendan."

"No, right now. Doc, that heifer is

really sick. She's valuable. Holstein she is, and a purebred. Her shoulder is swollen and black. Maybe she's got blackleg — "

Blackleg!

"Doc, you comin'?"

By this time, all vestiges of sleep had left Doc Jones. He lit the lamp, then said, "Hang on to your shirt, Brendan, and I'll open the door."

Brendan burst in, eyes wild and wide. He was about forty, with red, unruly hair.

"I milked as usual and put the cows out on their night pasture. The heifer had been layin' down all day. I looked her over and got her to her feet. She limped bad. Now her shoulder is swelled up awful big."

Doc Jeff, pulling on his socks, listened.

Lamplight showed the strained face of the farmer. "You think she has blackleg, Doc Jeff?"

"I don't know. Did you look at her hoofs?"

"I looked at both front hoofs. Not a rock wedged into them, Doc. Man, I cain't afford to lose that heifer."

Doc Jeff pulled on his pants and said consolingly, "We might be able to save her. I'll know more when I look at her." Dressed, he walked to a desk, pulled open a drawer, and took out a syringe. Then he got a vial of vaccine from the shelf.

All the while, Brendan had watched closely, eyes missing nothing.

"What you aim to do to her, Doc?"

"If she has blackleg, I'll shoot some vaccine into her. Might save her, but it might be too late."

Doggedly, the farmer shook his head. "I don't go for that stuff. I've read about it. When you do thet, you shoot germs into a livin' body. In my book, thet ain't good."

"Throw your book away."

"I mean thet, Doc Jeff. I don't crave to have germs shot into that heifer. Germs is bad. She's full of them now if'n she has blackleg."

103

Jeff studied him. "You mean that, Brendan?"

"I sure do."

Jeff appraised the man's stubbornness and knew it anchored in ignorance.

"You stupid, good-for-nothing fool! It isn't enough that I have to fight Endicott and Wheeler, but I have to fight ignorance, too! You wake me up and ask for help! Then you don't want my professional skill. Now get your rump outa here before I kick it out!"

Brendan's eyes glistened, and he wet his lips.

"Get out!" Doc Jeff ordered.

Suddenly, the farmer's stubbornness broke. "Doc Jeff, I'm just a igerant man, so don't go too tough on me. I'll take back what I said. I got to save that heifer. If germs'll do it, then into her them germs get shot!"

Jeff's anger subsided. This man was not to be censored; he was to be pitied. He knew little. The world, to him, was a small place.

"All right, Brendan. We ride."

"Thanks, Doc Jeff!"

Within ten minutes, they were loping toward the farmer's spread. Brendan took the lead through the sagebrush. Gradually, Doc Jeff's eyes became accustomed to the darkness. His horse was sure-footed, and Doc Jeff let him run free.

Brendan knew the way home. He headed straight for Wild Horse Flat with the surety of a homing pigeon. He also rode fast. Jeff's bronc had to push himself to stay up with the farmer's.

They swept along a ridge spiked with scrub pine that cast a pine odor into the night. Suddenly, Brendan reined in, bronc rising against the bit. From this high point, the basin lay below. And, to the north, there was a red tongue against the darkness, a licking and hungry tongue of bright redness.

"Fire, Doc!"

Doc Jeff Jones's mount skidded to a halt, and the veterinarian stared at the fire, something cold and deadly inside him.

Brendan hollered, "That's the house of thet new nester, the single gent that settled on the alkali beds. He jes' finished thet house two days ago. All of us farmers pitched in to help him!"

"Tough luck," Doc Jeff said.

"He ain't got a bit of water, either. Done dug a well by hand. Went over fifty feet without hittin' a trace of water."

"That is no farming country. A man can't raise wheat on an alkali bed, Brendan."

"Matt Wheeler says you can. Matt Wheeler says — "

"To heck with Wheeler. He's makin' fools out of you sodmen."

"He's our friend. Lends us money — "

"We'd best head over toward that fire," Jeff said. No use arguing with a man as ignorant as Brendan. "He might have got caught inside the house, and we might get him out if such is the case."

"By gosh, thet's right, Doc Jeff."

This time, Jeff's bronc took the lead.

He pointed the horse toward the fire about two miles away. They roared across a mesa dotted with greasewood and sagebrush. Behind Jeff, the farmer let his quirt rise and fall. Gradually, as they neared the fire, the flames became higher and bigger.

Without warning, Doc Jeff curbed his mount, the bronc coming to a halt with lunging, sliding jerks.

"Hold in, farmer!"

Brendan jerked his mount to a dust-scattering halt.

"Riders somewhere ahead, Brendan. I can hear them."

Brendan cocked his head, hand behind an ear. "Probably other farmers headin' in to help," he said. He raised his voice in loud hello. "This is Brendan an Doc Jones, ridin' in to help."

Brendan had made a serious error. For the riders were not heading toward the burning cabin; they were drifting away from it. Suddenly, they roared out of the night, hoofs jarring Montana sod — indistinct men riding shadowy horses toward them.

A gun roared, the flame beautiful against the darkness. Another gun talked, wicked and savage; it exploded three times. If any of the bullets came close, Doc Jeff did not hear them because of the roar of the six-shooters.

His own gun out, the vet piled to the ground, .45 raised. The mysterious riders passed about fifty yards away, and he shot twice. Each shot, though, was a guess shot, not accurately placed because the riders rode fast; he could barely make out their outline in the dark. Then the riders were in a ravine, out of sight.

Brendan's fingers were talons on Doc Jeff's arm. "Them wasn't farmers, Doc Jeff. Them was night raiders headin' away from a cabin they burned. Three of them, weren't they?"

Doc Jeff stood up, punching spent cartridge cases from his smoking .45. "Looked like about three to me," he admitted. "But the night is so dark . . . Might have been more. Could you identify any of them?"

"Not in this dark. Not even to their hosses."

Jeff swung into saddle, .45 now in leather. "We'd best head out, for that place didn't accidentally catch fire. Those riders set it on fire, unless I'm wrong."

"Endicott men," the farmer grunted. "Signing the articles of war by firin' one of our men's cabin and belongings!"

"Maybe those weren't Quarter Circle U riders," Doc Jeff hollered.

"Who else would set a farmer's spread on fire?"

Doc Jeff had no logical reply to that. "Maybe we're both wrong. Maybe the house caught fire accidentally."

Brendan rode close. "Them raiders sure unlimbered short-guns in a hurry. Good luck they were riding so fast, or we might've got plugged. This is range war, Doc Jeff."

"You scared?"

"Well, if it weren't for Wheeler an'

Osborne backin' us farmers, we'd be buckin' the tiger all alone. Wheeler says — "

Doc Jeff pushed ahead, and Brendan's horse caught him.

"The bullets scared the daylights outa me, Doc Jeff."

Again Doc Jeff had no answer to that, either. Had those riders really been Endicott Quarter Circle U men? How had blackleg germs got on this range? Was somebody contaminating the grass with blackleg germs? Who?

Who would win with blackleg? Surely not Endicott. Had he vaccinated his young stock, then secretly taken in an animal sick with blackleg to contaminate the farmers' unvaccinated herds — well, he could have won that way. For with the cattle of the farmers dead, they would have to leave, and the Quarter Circle U, following this line of logic, would again hold its old range.

Suddenly the burning house was ahead. Against the flames, Doc Jeff saw the figures of men, and he also saw the glitter of flames on rifles and pistols. Evidently, some of the nearby farmers had already reached the scene of the fire.

Brendan hollered, "Brendan and Doc Jeff coming in, men. Hold your fire, 'cause we're your friends!"

"Come on in, men!"

Their broncs skidded to a stop, and again boots hit the ground. Farmers gathered around them, and the flame of the building reflected on their savage faces.

"Not a drop of water on the place," a farmer said. "Ed here almost got burned in his shack."

The owner had escaped with only his underwear. He stood barefooted, hair tousled.

"Accident?" Doc Jeff asked.

"Accident, heck! Kerosene was spread all over the outside — right above the foundation. The crackle of the flames luckily awoke me. When I ran outside, the entire base of the house was on fire."

"Can you prove kerosene?"

"I smelled it."

A man came running with a five-gallon can. "Found this in the brush, men! The can what had the kerosene in it. My Gawd, look at this sign painted on it. The Quarter Circle U brand!"

"What?"

"Endicott's work," a man snarled. "We oughta ride over to that spread and take it apart, timber by timber, an' burn it to the ground."

"We shot it out with three riders that almost run over us," Brendan informed them. "They was headin' toward the Endicott spread, too. Bet it was Mike Endicott and two of his gunmen!"

"You did what?"

While Brendan excitedly told his story, Doc Jeff circled the burning building, looking for more clues. The farmers stood in a group and talked in loud, demanding voices against the Quarter Circle U. The can went from one farmer to the other, each giving it minute and useless examination.

One farmer, a bowlegged fellow Jeff had met once or twice, came over to where Jeff stood looking at the dying flames.

"What do you say, Doc Jeff?"

"Nice cool night."

"Heck, I don't mean about the night. I mean, what do you think about Mike Endicott deliberately burnin' down this building? He might've killed Ed in the flames. Then it would have been murder. Endicott — "

"Maybe Endicott didn't do it."

The man peered at him, instantly belligerent. "How can you talk that way? Endicott hates us farmers. He claims openly he has to git rid of us. If he didn't do it, who did?"

Doc Jeff had a few pet theories of his own. But he knew better than to tip his hand to this belligerent farmer. The way he figured it, Matt Wheeler had some of his men on homesteads, stool pigeons for him. This man, whose name was Barclay, might be a Wheeler man, masquerading as a farmer to get inside dope on the way the hoemen regarded Wheeler and Osborne.

"Forget it, Barclay."

"I ain't forgettin' it, though. I don't like what you implied, hoss doctor. I agree with Matt Wheeler. I still think you favor Endicott because he's got lots of cattle and hosses and can give you more trade than us poor farmers with only a few head of cattle! I still agree with Wheeler when he says — "

"Close your big mouth!"

Barclay came forward, fists doubled. Jeff had had enough. He threw out a hard right that crashed through Barclay's guard. He heard the man grunt, felt him go back a pace; he moved in, working both fists in solid satisfaction. He knocked Barclay down.

"Get up if you feel lucky."

Already farmers had moved between them. Brendan helped Barclay to his feet, and Jeff, fists still doubled, watched the farmer wipe blood from his mouth. He spat and glared at

Doc Jeff, the flames showing the evil darkness of his narrowed eyes.

Brendan said, "I figger you owe Doc Jeff a apology, Barclay. You accused him unjustly, I figure. He's ridin' with me now to doctor a sick heifer of mine. And me, I ain't got but a few bucks to pay with, if he'll split my last two bucks with me."

"I won't apologize — "

Another man said, "You doubled your fists first, fella. Doc Jeff hit in self-defense. He might be against us farmers, but I'm for fair play."

Barclay spat again. "I'll see him in hell first," he said angrily.

Brendan said slowly, "You're plumb wrong, Barclay." He looked at Doc Jeff Jones. "Nothin' we kin do here, Doc Jeff. We might as well drift out to my place and see thet heifer."

Jeff shrugged, then grinned and stepped into leather. He and Brendan rode out, leaving the farmers behind, and from a ridge he looked back at the knotted group, wondering what plan of action they would take. If they raided the Quarter Circle U, they would run into lead and flame, and some of their women who were now wives would be widows come daylight. He hoped they would not listen to hotheads like Barclay.

"Thet kerosene can clinches it against the Endicott spread," Brendan hollered above the pound of hoofs. "Tomorrow mornin' that no-good deputy of a Chuck Coogan will have thet can shoved into his hands whether he likes it or not. But he won't do nothin'."

"Looks awful like a setup deal to me," Jeff said.

"Not to me. They had to leave so fast, they just forgot the can, that's all. Either that, or it fell off a saddle, 'cause it was found in the bresh a ways from the cabin."

"Accidents can happen," Jeff had to admit.

Dawn was moving across this wide wilderness when they rode down off the hills and into the yard of the Brendan farm.

Mrs. Brendan, a heavyset young woman, came out carrying a dishpan full of water, which she spilled on the ground. Wiping her red hands on her apron, she put the pan on a bench beside the log cabin and came toward them as they dismounted in front of the sod barn.

"The heifer's in the barn, men."

Brendan said seriously, "The Quarter Circle U burned down Barclay's new house, Anna."

"They what?"

Doc Jeff left them talking about the fire. The heifer was tied to a stall. It was very dark inside the sod barn, and the animal lay on its side.

Doc Jones led the animal outside. Both Brendans now gave him and the heifer their full attention. Doc Jeff knew, at first glance, that the animal had blackleg. Still, he felt its shoulder and noticed the well-developed area of swelling, the crackling of the black and distended hide over its shoulders.

Brendan spoke haltingly. "What's the matter with her, Doc Jeff?"

"Blackleg."

His wife repeated, "Blackleg? I can't believe it. Where would she get blackleg?"

"From one of your other cows, or somebody else's cows. A cow can be a carrier and still not show symptoms of the disease. Or she might have got it from the grass. Anyway, she has it — and has it bad."

"She won't live?" the woman asked, voice hollow.

"Vaccine might save her. But it could be too late."

Brendan spoke to his wife. "That means shootin' germs into her," he explained. "Remember, we read about it, and the magazine was against it."

Doc Jones was in the act of untying his bag from his saddle. He stopped, let his hands fall, and studied the couple.

"That ain't right," the wife said hotly. "I'm not fer it, husband. That is poisonin' a critter with more germs, I'd say."

Jeff waited, feeling a knife's edge of patience. The dean at the school had been right: ignorance was the world's worst enemy.

"I told him that, Anna."

"The heifer ain't gonna git thet needle, Doc Jeff," she said.

"She'll die then."

"I don't believe it. The Almighty never made it that way."

Doc Jeff looked at her, then at Brendan. Futility rolled across him, mirroring itself in his thin face.

"The rest of your young cattle will get the disease," he said evenly. "Let me vaccinate them and save them. I'll admit that vaccine might come too late to save this nice heifer."

"None of them," the woman said stoutly, "will feel that terrible needle. Germs shot into a livin' body — None of that, Doc Jeff."

Doc Jones looked again at Terry Brendan. The rancher's lips were set, his mind made up, and this radiated from the fixed expression on his wife's face.

Doc Jeff said, "Your neighbors' cattle will get it, too. You'll be the cause of your neighbors' losses."

"We'll wait an' see for sure."

Doc Jeff said slowly, "Someday there'll be a law that will make you vaccinate young stock against diseases. Society has to be protected against the stupidity and ignorance of people of your low intelligence."

Brendan stepped forward a pace, fists knotted. "Don't insult me an' my wife jes' 'cause you went to college."

"Back at that fire, you told the men you had two bucks. You offered to pay me one buck — to split the pot. But you aren't splitting it, savvy? You got me out here, out of bed, to look at this heifer. I looked at her and could possibly save her except for your ignorance. I'm getting your two bucks, Brendan."

"You are like — "

120

"Unless you pay me, I'll whip the living daylights out of you."

Brendan eyed him, then stepped back a pace. Deliberately, he spread out his hands to show he did not want to fight. He was shaking.

"Give him the money, Terry," the wife said. "You're no fist-fighter. All the boys back in Indiana used to whup you."

Brendan dug into his pocket. He gave Doc Jeff two bucks. The vet mounted, looked down, said, "Thanks." His voice was sarcastic.

Then his bronc, lunging ahead, kicked gravel into the faces of Mr. and Mrs. Terry Brendan . . .

8

THE pitch-black darkness of a Montana night. The jar of thundering hoofs smashing through sagebrush and greasewood Three broncs that followed no trail across the flats. And big Matt Wheeler, riding at the point of his two men, opened the loading gate of his .45.

Even in the inky darkness, he could load and empty the big Colt. Now he punched out the cases of the fired cartridges, and his blunt fingers crammed in fresh shells. He clicked shut the heavy loading gate and restored the big gun to the oiled holster tied to his thigh.

Twisting on stirrups, the land-locater looked back, but the dark night had claimed the two riders.

"Who was them two horsemen, Lee?"

"I sure dunno, boss. They jus' come outa the night."

"One looked like the vet to me," Miller said. "Looked like Doc Jones, or I'm a plumb bad guess."

"He's home in bed," Lee Osborne snarled. "You talk like a loco man, George. Well, one thing is certain — we never recognized them, an' that means they couldn't recognize us."

"Sure looked like Doc Jones," George Miller said doggedly. "And that other one — he looked like Terry Brendan to me. Same build as Brendan."

Matt Wheeler pulled his bronc to a sudden halt. "Wait a minute," he said hoarsely. "Maybe George is right. Maybe it was the vet and Terry Brendan at that."

"I got good eyes," boasted George Miller. "Even in the dark I kin see good. I'm sartain they was them two — Doc Jeff an' Terry Brendan."

"It does make sense," Lee Osborne grudgingly asserted.

"How come it make sense?" George

Miller looked at one man, then the other. But the night hid their features.

Matt Wheeler seemed to be talking to himself. "Sure as shootin', that was the vet and Terry Brendan. That means that the blackleg germs have done their work in Brendan's pasture. He rode to town for Doc, and they saw the fire and headed that way to see if they could help."

"That should be the deal," Lee Osborne said.

George Miller asked, "What you two talkin' about?"

Again Wheeler's voice droned, "And by bad luck, we happened to run into each other, and on a night this dark — Talk about coincidence . . . "

"Brendan might want to vaccinate, but his wife is dead set against it," Lee Osborne said slowly. "We sounded her and him out good on that point. She won't let that Doc put a hypo in her animals."

"Let's hope not," Matt Wheeler said.

"You two," declared George Miller,

"are talkin' in riddles."

"To you, yes," said Matt Wheeler. "And what's more, you can stay on the merry-go-round, Miller. The less you know, the better off you'll be."

"I only work for wages, boss."

"Remember that, and keep your mouth shut."

"Hell is gonna bust loose," Miller said. "That kerosene can will be the match and the fuse and the black powder all in one."

"Within twenty four hours," said Matt Wheeler, "this range will be a range of death — blackleg death. Come on, men, and ride!"

They headed out again, a trio of hard-riding horsemen. Wheeler's plan called for them to be in Scrub Pine before daylight. Then nobody would ever know whether or not they had been out of their beds that night. But dawn was close, for the night had slipped by rapidly.

Osborne put his bronc close to that of his boss. His chuckle was as dry as the rustle of fall leaves.

"That contaminated cowhide sure did the work, boss. The germs sure must've liked it. From where did you say you shipped in that cowhide, Wheeler?"

"I told you once. From down in Wyoming. It came from somewhere around Lander. They've had blackleg hard in that section. I got a friend to peel me the hide off a yearling steer that had just died from blackleg."

"That sure puts the germs in the grass, eh?"

"Enough of that. Keep Miller in ignorance."

George Miller mocked, "Poor ol' Miller. George is the given name. Keep him in ignorance. Only don't forget to pay him good, Wheeler."

Wheeler smiled with his lips only. In the first touch of dawn, his eyes were dead and dull.

They rode in silence for a mile; then Osborne said, "Endicott's bull should be dead by now."

"Should be."

"What if Doc Jeff Jones sends out for vaccine? How about the vaccine in his office?"

"I'll tend to those points."

Osborne suddenly held up his hand, and the horses skidded to a halt.

"What's wrong, Lee?" demanded Wheeler, his voice hoarse.

Lee Osborne canted his heavy head, lips slightly apart. "I hear riders comin' this way."

Miller growled, "I don't hear none."

"Me, either," Wheeler said.

Osborne kept his head twisted, listening. "A bunch of 'em, too. Headin' this way, comin' from the direction of the Quarter Circle U outfit!"

Miller said, "I can't hear — "

Wheeler cut in with, "He's right. Comin' this way. Yonder's a coulee — hit it, men!"

The coulee was about two hundred yards away, a gash in the earth's tanned crust. They took it on the run, spilling down into it. It was rather shallow, though. Bullberry bushes and serviceberry trees were in it, and these, along with the depression of the soil, hid them and their broncs.

They dismounted, rifles in hand, then went ahead on foot, climbing the slope down which they had so hurriedly ridden. There, hidden by the rim-rock, they watched the riders sweep by, dim and uncertain outlines against the flickering dawn. A gaunt man rode in the lead of about ten men, a man who rode high on the stirrups, fitting his muscles to the lope of his bronc with the long ease of a man born to saddle leather.

Wheeler breathed, "Mike Endicott."

"Ridin' toward the nester house," Lee Osborne said. "And for why, Matt?"

George Miller answered. "Mebbe Endicott figures all the farmers will be at the fire, an' he an' his men can ride down an' circle them and kill them off all at once."

"Could be," Lee Osborne agreed.

Wheeler shook his head. "I doubt if Mike would take such a tough step right off the bat. More than likely he's afraid the fire might turn into a prairie fire and burn off his grass."

"He might get his whiskers singed," Lee Osborne said. "Them farmers ain't gonna take too kindly to him and his crew ridin' in at a moment like this. What say we trail them and see what busts loose, Matt?"

"Somebody might glimpse us," Wheeler said. "We don't want to be seen on this part of the range at this time, Lee."

"I'd sure like to see the mess," Miller said.

"We ride to town," Wheeler ordered.

The last of the Quarter Circle U men rounded the toe of the hill, and then there were only the sounds of horse's hoofs; finally these died out against the distance. By now, the three were mounted, riding toward Scrub Pine.

Matt Wheeler was lost in his thoughts.

They were, for the most part, comforting thoughts. They were good because they centered around one word: money. He wanted deeds — legal deeds — to this range. He made money locating the farmers. Sooner or later the farmers would have to leave their homesteads. Poor soil. No rain. They were mostly city men hoping to escape factory work by becoming farmers. They knew nothing about farming. When they had starved enough, they would gladly sell their deeds to him for a few dollars.

By now, he and Lee Osborne should have been safe in South America. Time was running against them. You don't rob a bank and kill a banker without having the Pinkertons on your trail . . . But the loot from that bank was chicken feed compared with the loot that lay here in the dry bosom of Scrub Pine range. This loot would be cut three ways. One third to Osborne, a third for him, and a third for the geologist down in Denver.

It had all happened unexpectedly.

He and Osborne had been living in an obscure Denver hotel. They had met a man who was a geologist and had become somewhat chummy. They had had drinks together; the geologist got too drunk. He had talked, and a deal had been made.

Wheeler had looked up the geologist's credentials. He was all that he professed to be. He was, in fact, a genius, but he could not leave whiskey alone. Had he been sober, he would have never told them about Scrub Pine's treasure.

Scrub Pine belonged to the government, and, as the geologist stressed, a man couldn't lease government land. There was only one way to get control of Scrub Pine: to move in farmers, get them to homestead, then get them to leave after selling their homestead rights. The geologist had also told them about blackleg. He had, in fact, thought of the original plan: get farmers settled, then kill off their stock with blackleg. The loss of their cattle would make them leave faster.

Now Doc Jeff Jones the veterinarian had moved in. And if Doc Jeff held down blackleg, their plan would be slowed down to a walk. Doc Jeff had to go.

Another thought came to Wheeler: '*You don't have to kill Doc Jeff. Just keep him out of vaccine. It isn't the man himself you are fighting at this time, but you have to keep him from using vaccine against blackleg.*'

Miller, by drinking too much, had almost queered their plan. There rose in Matt Wheeler at this moment an intense hatred for George Miller. When the man drank, he talked too much; he knew too much to talk about.

He reined close to Miller's bronc. "Miller, what's over there in the sagebrush?"

Miller turned his head to look.

Wheeler's .45 hit Miller across the base of the skull. He threw up his hands and fell hard out of saddle, landing on the ground.

Osborne's eyes widened. "What the — "

Matt Wheeler was out of saddle. "He knows too much." He beat Miller's head with his gun barrel. Miller lay silent and still. Wheeler was panting as he beat the man's head again.

Osborne said, "He's dead, Matt."

Wheeler straightened, his breath tearing out of him. "He knew too much," he repeated. "He talked too much, too. He won't talk now."

Osborne wet his lips. He felt cold, suddenly, and shaky. The dark and terrible rage mirrored on Wheeler's face disturbed him.

Wheeler found his stirrup and mounted. He holstered his .45 and looked down at the man who but a few moments before had ridden beside him.

"What do we do with him?" Osborne asked.

"Nothing."

"We leave him there?"

"Sure, why not? Let the blame fall

on the vet. Him an' Miller had a row, remember? Maybe the vet met him and they fought and the vet killed him."

"Maybe so." Osborne grinned.

"Leave his bronc here, too," Wheeler said. "Come on, Lee."

They strung out again, Wheeler leading the way, Osborne close at his right. Osborne trembled. He remembered the bloody head of the dead man. He remembered the look of terrible ferocity on Matt Wheeler's face. Wheeler would kill him just as readily when and if the proper time came.

"Darn it, Matt, but you sure kilt him easy."

"A man dies easily. You oughta know that. One bullet, and that banker keeled over — remember how he died? Remember his eyes?"

"For God's sake, shut your mouth. We both killed him."

Wheeler almost smiled at that. "Blame equal on both of us," he affirmed. "Hope the blame for this gets on the doc."

"Hope so, too."

Osborne put his bronc even with Matt Wheeler's. He had never trusted Wheeler, but never before had he seen the man make such a violent and deadly decision. He decided that, from here on, his back would never be to Wheeler and that when they rode, he would keep his horse at a far distance for safety. And he would not ride ahead of Wheeler, either.

9

WHEN Doc Jeff Jones reached town, anger against the Brendan tribe had left him. He was dog-tired, for the day before had been a busy one, so he went immediately to bed.

His sleep was of short duration, however, for again hammering knuckles on his door dragged him slowly awake. Had Brendan changed his mind and come into town for him again?

"Who's there?"

"Hank Nelson."

"What do you want?"

"Four of my yearlin' are down. Can't get up! Shoulders are stiff, Doc. Never have seen blackleg, but it looks like blackleg to me — "

Doc Jones sat up in bed, the words driving energy into him. He crossed the room and unlocked the door.

136

Hank Nelson had a black eye. His lips were puffed, and one ear had blood on it — dried blood.

"What happened to you, Nelson?"

"Fight."

"Your old lady must have a powerful left hook."

The Norwegian grinned. "Sadie didn't do it, Doc. After you left the cabin, the Endicott gang came over, and we all fought a prairie fire; then we had a fight — us farmers against them!"

"I'd sure liked to have seen that! All of you fight, the — gang fight?"

"We sure did. But that's neither here nor there. My young stock is down — I know it's blackleg."

Doc Jeff Jones sat down on the bed. Things had happened fast, and he needed a little time to adjust his sleepy brain to the problem at hand.

"Lord, what a night, eh?"

Nelson grinned crookedly. "We had a lot of fun. Endicott claims that can was stolen from his spread and put by that burnin' shack as a method to lay the blame for the fire on him. What do you think about that, Doc?"

"Might be."

"Might not be the truth, too. What you gonna do to them cows of mine?"

"Vaccinate them."

The farmer scowled. "Thet means you shoot germs into a livin' body, don't it, Doc?"

"Yes. Do we have to go through that again? Brendan is losing his cattle because he won't let me vaccinate. Now, don't tell me you're that bullheaded and stupid, Nelson?"

Nelson debated, eyes hard and shiny. "I don't like the idea."

"Idea of what?"

"Like I said. Shootin' them germ things into a livin' hunk of meat."

Doc Jeff lay on his bunk. He put his hands under his head and looked at the ceiling. "Let your stock die, then. Now you get outa of here pronto!" He rolled over and faced the wall. "I want to get some sleep."

The farmer did not move. Doc Jeff

rolled over and looked at Nelson. The man's face, beaten and swollen, showed his struggle — the struggle of ignorance against possible financial loss. Nelson's lips moved, and he swallowed.

Doc Jeff said, "Did you hear me?"

The man's lips trembled. "I rode past Brendan's place. He told me to tell you thet his sick cow died."

"He wouldn't let me vaccinate."

"That bull of Endicott's — the one you said had blackleg — is alive, and you never vaccinated him."

So Ma Endicott had vaccinated the bull and saved him, Doc Jeff thought. And because she had saved him, he would have to pay the price of having diagnosed a blackleg wrongly. Endicott would crow to the high heavens that he was the worst vet to come down the pike. Was anything going to work out?

"Why do you smile, Doc?"

"I'm smiling at your ignorance. Again, get out — or make up your mind!"

"Endicott wouldn't let you vaccinate

his bull. So . . . the bull is alive and gettin' well. Brendan wouldn't let you shoot germs into his heifer. She died. Me, I don't see — "

"Are you, or aren't you?"

"I don't see — "

Jeff got to his feet, fists up. "Nelson, I'm going to heave you out of my office, and do it bodily! And when I throw you into the alley, you won't land gently, either. You rode in for my services. Do you want my professional skill, or do you want another fist-fight?"

Nelson drew back, arms up. "Doc, don't hit! Come out and vaccinate if it will save my cattle! Vaccinate them all, Doc!"

"Your greed got the best of your prejudices, eh?"

"Them words is too big for me, Doc. I'm sorry for what I said an' did. Get some vaccination stuff an ride with me."

"That's better." Jeff pulled on his boots. "I'll get some chuck first. I'm hungry. A few minutes' delay won't make much difference." He eyed the man coldly. "Remember this always — the vaccine might not work. It might be too late; the cattle might be too sick. But if I don't vaccinate, they all die."

"The bull didn't."

"T'heck with that bull!"

Dressed, Doc Jeff went through the curtain that divided his sleeping quarters from his laboratory and office. He kept his vaccine on a high shelf. He got a chair and stood on it while Nelson watched, mouth open. Evidently, the array of bottles and vials impressed the ignorant farmer deeply.

Doc Jeff said, "What the heck?"

"What's the matter?"

"My blackleg vaccine vials are gone."

"They're what?"

"You heard me. They're gone."

"Maybe you moved them and forgot where you put them."

Jeff shook his head. Something was decidedly wrong here. The vaccine bottles had been in their proper places yesterday when he had taken the hypodermic needle and vial out to Ma Endicott.

Dust that had collected on the shelf was disturbed by the rings made by the vials. Somebody, he realized, had been in his office while he had ridden to the Brendan farm. But the door had been locked and the windows hooked shut.

He ran to a window, the office had two of them. The first was locked securely, but the hook had been broken on the other. He opened it hurriedly and looked at the sill. There, in the soft wood, was the imprint of a crowbar, a crowbar that had pried open the window, breaking the hook!

"Somebody has busted in here," Nelson said.

Jeff nodded. "Wonderful deduction, Nelson." He tried to keep the irony from his voice. "Looks to me like somebody wants the cattle around here to die from blackleg."

"Must've been Endicott or one of his men."

Doc Jeff studied the farmer. "What makes your mind reach such a conclusion, Nelson?"

"Well, if us farmers lose all our stock, we'll have to leave the country, and who profits if we pull out for good?" He answered that with one word: "Endicott!"

Doc Jeff said scornfully, "Great logic. But did it ever occur to you that Endicott would lose lots of cattle, too? Blackleg will hit his herds, too."

"I know that. I'm not that dumb. But there's one angle you've overlooked, Doc Jeff."

"What?"

"Maybe Endicott has vaccinated his animals on the sly. Then, with his herds safe, he got in blackleg germs to kill off our stock."

"That isn't true."

"How do you know?"

"That bull had blackleg. Had Endicott vaccinated his young stock on spring roundup, the bull would not have got sick."

"Maybe the bull never had blackleg! He never died, Doc Jeff. You diagnosed his case plumb wrong, us farmers think."

Doc Jeff Jones had to smile again, ruefully. The bull, figuratively speaking, had reversed the usual position. Instead of his having the bull by the horns, the bull was giving him a rough time. And he dare not say that Ma Endicott had vaccinated the Quarter Circle U bull. To do so would bring down the wrath of Mike Endicott on her graying head.

"I guess I did."

"You sure side with Mike Endicott in this deal, eh, Doc Jeff? Is that 'cause he has more cattle than us farmers?"

Doc Jeff had heard enough. He grabbed Nelson unexpectedly, got a hammer lock on the man, and propelled him urgently through the door. Nelson hit the alley and fell on his face. He got up rubbing his arm.

"You got a awful temper, Doc Jeff!"

"Come back when you can talk sense, you bonehead sodman!" He shut the door, leaving Nelson in the alley. His wrestling experience, gained in college, had come in handy.

His mind returned to his vaccine. Somebody had stolen it, and had not touched another thing in his office. He again stood on the chair, looking at the shelf and its telltale dust rings. Then, to make sure, he methodically searched his office for the vaccine. But to no avail. Somebody had stolen it. Somebody wanted the sick cattle to die. But who had done it? George Miller? He didn't know.

Miller had worked for Wheeler. Did that mean then, that Wheeler didn't want the cattle saved? Or that maybe the land-locater figured only Mike Endicott's cattle should remain unvaccinated? There was something more to this, something hidden. Doc Jeff, standing there in his office, let his mind wonder. Was there something under the ground that Wheeler and Osborne wanted?

Nelson stuck in his head with, "Me, I don't hold no grudge, Doc Jeff. I'm gonna leg it over and talk this over with Matt Wheeler and Lee Osborne. They're friends to us farmers, our only friends — "

"Very staunch friends," Doc Jeff said ironically.

Nelson overlooked that. "Why don't you order some vaccination stuff, Doc Jeff? Where do you order it from, and how long will it take to get here?"

"By the time it got here, your cattle would be dead and burned, Nelson. I have to order it from Helena, the capital."

Nelson scowled. "Long way off, and trains are slow. Lord, this is a mess — I'm gonna talk with Wheeler about it!"

"Send the deputy sheriff over, if you see him."

"All right."

Doc Jeff went down the alley and

entered the Branding Iron Cafe by the back door. Millie was cooking hotcakes over the big range.

"Somebody broke into my office last night," he told her, "and stole all my blackleg vaccine. Almost every young cow on the range is down."

"They what?"

"That's it," Jeff said, sitting on a stool.

"Who did it, Jeff?"

"I don't know. Wheeler and Osborne, I think. They got some deep and dark plan, and because I'm a vet, I'm tangled up in it. Somebody shot at me an Brendan last night. Three riders in the dark, looked like. Lucky we never stopped a bullet. Then the Endicott riders tangled with the farmers at the burning house."

"I heard about that. Must've been a battle royal."

Doc Jeff stood up. "Wish I knew, for sure, which side I was fighting. I'm getting a little mad. I'd like to make some fur fly off'n somebody.

Endicott is against me, so are Wheeler and Osborne, and the farmers think I'm a quack." He showed his boyish smile. "Maybe I am at that."

"You are not. Have breakfast with me?"

"Haven't got time, honey. Coogan should be at my office now. He isn't much, but he's the law, and he has to be paid some respect."

"He rode out to the scene of the fight, they tell me. He should be in soon, though. This heat will drive him in. He hates the heat."

"Lots of things he hates," Doc Jeff said slowly.

Her eyes showed something. Was it worry for him? He hoped so. Then he remembered his financial condition.

"Take care of yourself, Doc Jeff."

"I'll be back," he promised.

He returned to his office. A farmer awaited him there. The farmer had six head of heifers and steers, and all were down with what looked like blackleg. The other farmers so far had objected to vaccination. Well, he didn't object a bit if vaccination would save his stock.

"Somebody broke into my office and stole my vaccine."

"They what?"

Sitting on a chair and looking idly at his boots, the farmer's eyes almost left his homely head.

"Endicott — or some of his hands — stole it, Doc Jeff."

"What makes you say that?"

"Endicott would profit if us farmers had to leave. He might have vaccinated his stock on spring roundup without us knowing about it, then he might have planted blackleg germs on this grass so our cows would die."

Doc Jeff asked, almost wearily, "How could he plant the germs, Walker?"

"Doc Jeff, I'm no ordinary farmer. For five years, I done tracked down Apaches, down in Arizony — workin' for Uncle Sam's army. And I know a sign when I see it, fella. And I've done seen some sign, too, believe you me!"

Jeff's surprise was genuine. "Well, I'll be hanged!" He had taken this hulking man to be only a farmer, nothing more. "Go on, Walker, you talk interesting. What sign did you see?"

Walker claimed that somebody had dragged a cowhide or some other wide surface over his pasture. "A couple of gents has rid acrost my grass, draggin' somethin' behin' their hosses, Doc Jeff. Couldn't've been very heavy 'cause it only bent the grass over a little bit, and the grass soon come almost straight up again."

Doc Jeff nodded, giving this some thought. Maybe this farmer had stumbled on something big.

"Could them draggin' a cowhide acrost my grass — a dried-out cowhide — give the grass them blackleg germs?"

"It sure could," Doc Jeff Jones agreed. "But maybe you read the sign wrong, Walker?"

"I've done trailed Apaches an' Navajos, and I kin read sign. Them

Quarter Circle U cowpokes has done it. Endicott wants us hoemen out so he can run cattle again on grass we've done put under fence."

"I don't know," Doc Jeff said. "I'm not Mike Endicott. But I do know this thing has sure got me in the middle. Everybody is out to nail my hide to the fence. Somebody even shot at me and Brendan last night. I had two fights yesterday, and Miller swore to kill me, they tell me."

"You gonna order some more vaccine, Doc Jeff?"

"I sure am if the wholesale company will ship it out on credit. I have darned little money. If the farmers had any brains, they'd build up a pool of money to tide us over this emergency."

"Us farmers ain't got much money. Well, looks like *this* man is already out of the farming business. Wonder if Wheeler will buy my deed?"

"Yeah, at his price."

Walker seemed to have consoled himself to face his loss. "Wheeler sure is a friend of us farmers. He hated Endicott. Says the only reason he buys these homestead rights is to keep them away from Mike Endicott."

"That's nice of Wheeler," Doc Jones said wryly.

Walker went down the alley, heading for Wheeler's office. Doc Jones sat and contemplated a week-old newspaper. He was not interested in it, though. He kept remembering the riders roaring out of the night, the spit of guns against himself and Terry Brendan.

Deputy Sheriff Coogan came in, all business. "Was out investigatin' that fire, Doc Jeff. Talked to almost all the farmers and to Endicott. Endicott claims he never set it, even if there was a five-gallon kerosene can found with his brand painted on it. Reckon they had quite a tussle when them boys started scrappin'. Had I been there, I'd've stopped that fight pronto."

Amused, Doc Jeff nodded.

"Some of the farmers want me to arrest Mike Endicott. Arson, the charge. I don't know, though. Not enough evidence, I'd say."

"You wouldn't do that."

"If I had the evidence, I would!"

Doc Jeff shook his head. "Endicott is a political power, and he'd have your job inside of two days. He'd get word to the sheriff at the county seat, and Chuck Coogan would have to go back punching cows — if he could get the job."

Coogan hurried to change the subject. "Millie done said somebody had jimmied a window an sneaked in to steal your blackleg vaccine, Doc Jeff. That true?"

"That's right."

"I'll look around for clues."

Doc Jeff got to his feet. "You won't find any. Let's go down to the cafe and get some chuck."

"I just et."

"Another meal won't hurt you. My vaccine is gone. Somebody wants cows to die of blackleg."

"Don't seem reasonable that a man'd

deliberately make poor cattle suffer," the deputy said, shaking his head. "Who'd do that, Doc Jeff?"

"I got my own suspicions."

As they went outside and walked toward the Branding Iron Cafe, Deputy Sheriff Chuck Coogan, chewing tobacco with deliberate slowness, said, "They tell me thet George Miller has made threats against you, Doc Jeff. When I see him again, I'll warn him to keep his mug clamped shut."

"Where is he?"

"Ain't seen him since you done run him outa town."

They entered Millie's cafe and took stools near the door. Through the window they could see the main street.

Millie came to take their orders. Coogan ordered only coffee, but Doc Jones ordered a full breakfast with all the trimmings. He was finishing his hotcakes when three horses came down the main street. Two of the broncs were ridden by two Quarter Circle U men — Mike Endicott and a cowpuncher.

"What in the livin' — ?" Coogan was on his feet, going out the door, with Doc Jeff a pace behind him. "That third hoss has a dead man tied onto him, Doc Jeff. Somethin' sure went haywire again."

"Maybe he isn't dead," Doc Jeff said. "Maybe he's just wounded."

Mike Endicott hollered, "Hey, Coogan!"

The man lay jackknifed over the pack saddle. His head was bloody and beaten, and when Coogan pulled his head upward by the hair, Doc Jeff saw the man's face.

Behind him he heard Millie's excited, "That dead man is George Miller!"

Coogan let the head drop. Millie said, "I'm — I got to get back inside," and she scurried away. Doc Jeff realized that the sight of the man's broken-in face had made her sick.

Coogan looked up at Endicott. "What happened to Miller, Mike?"

Endicott moved his rawboned height on stirrups, and he looked at Doc

Jones. "I don't know what happened to Miller. Jim an' me was ridin' the South Fork range again, and we found him dead. Somebody must've beat him over the haid with a boulder. The rock was nearby. His hoss is at my ranch now."

"Wonder who killed him?"

"I dunno."

Mike Endicott was still looking at Doc Jones. Suddenly the vet was aware that all the onlookers were watching him closely. They had grown, all of a sudden, into a tight band of silent accusers, and their eyes were sharp and suspicious. Coogan said, "Well, he won't go against you now, Doc Jeff."

"Reckon not."

Coogan spoke to Endicott. "Take his carcass to that little building behind the Mercantile, Mike. Doc Jeff, come over to my office, please. I'd like to have a few words with you."

"As you say, Coogan."

The vet and the deputy walked off in silence. The onlookers followed

Endicott and his hired hand down the street. Once in his office, Coogan slammed his length into his swivel chair and leaned back.

"Doc Jeff, this looks bad for you."

Doc Jeff looked out the window, his face immobile. He decided to play ignorant. "I don't quite follow you, Coogan."

Coogan looked at him. "Don't joke with me, Doc Jeff."

Doc Jeff said, "All right, Miller is dead. Somebody clubbed him to death with a boulder. Endicott and his hand find him and bring in his body. What's that got to do with me, lawman?" His voice, despite his efforts, had become hard.

Coogan's long fingers drummed on the arms of his chair. "Miller made threats against you. He said he would kill you. Now, all of a sudden, Miller is dead."

"Good riddance, I'd say."

"I agree with you there. But the law cain't look upon the worth of a dead man. The law has to find his killer. Accordin' to Endicott, Miller's carcass was found between here and Terry Brendan's place."

"I get your point," Doc Jeff said. "But I didn't kill Miller. Terry Brendan and I shot at three midnight riders, but we didn't, to the best of our knowledge, down any of them. We might have hit one or more of them, though. I wonder if there was a bullet hole in Miller?"

Mike Endicott, who had just entered, answered that with, "No bullet holes, Doc Jeff. Just his head beat in."

"That kills the theory that either me or Brendan got a bullet into one of those riders . . . if Miller was one of those gunmen."

"You came to town from Brendan's homestead alone, eh?" Coogan asked.

"That I did. Alone."

"Too bad somebody didn't happen to ride with you; then you'd have had an airtight alibi."

"Heck, I never killed Miller!"

Coogan looked at Endicott, then

Endicott said, "I believe you, Doc Jeff. But these other people prob'ly don't, judgin' from the way they looked at you. I've heard talk. They got the theory you killed Miller because he threatened to kill you. They all remember that you came in from Brendan's this morning."

Doc Jeff nodded. "That's logical. What do you say, Coogan?"

"I don't think you did it, Doc Jeff. Looks to me like somebody come in from behind Miller an slugged him cold an' then whupped in his head. To beat a man with a rock, he has to be unconscious before the beatin' starts, I'd say."

"Sounds good to me," Endicott said.

"I'm goin' out there an' scout for clues," Coogan said, "and I want you with me, Endicott, to show me just how the body lay, and all that. And you, Doc Jeff, take it easy, stay out of trouble, and watch yourself."

"If you get in trouble," Mike Endicott said ironically, "I hope you can fist-fight better than you can diagnose the ailments of a cow. Thet bull you said would die is still alive, Doc Jeff, an' is gettin' better fast."

"That's good."

Scowling, Deputy Sheriff Coogan watched him, and his long, dirty fingers drummed on the arms of his swivel chair.

10

ACROSS the street, other fingers drummed on the arm of a chair — those of Matt Wheeler, who sat and looked through his broken window at Coogan's office.

"We've had some good luck for a change," Wheeler said.

Osborne was playing solitaire, cards spread on the dirty floor. "We need it, Matt."

"Heck, we've had good luck, Lee. We've got all of Doc Jones' vaccine, and blackleg's pretty well established on this grass."

"We could plant germs in some other places, Matt, to make darned sure all the cattle get it."

"We've got our farmers mad at the cowboys. That gang fight this morning made them hate each other even more," Wheeler replied.

"Miller blundered. That almost laid the finger on us, Wheeler. That fight with Doc Jones out in the lava beds did us no good, either."

"I thought he would talk sense, not fight."

"He didn't talk sense, though."

Wheeler continued with, "Well, Miller is dead now — he can't talk. These dumb clucks around this burg will swear that Miller was killed by Doc Jeff Jones, which is the way we want it."

"Luck, Matt."

"Miller was just another drifter when he was alive, but now that he's dead, he's suddenly everybody's friend."

"What is crazier than people, Matt?"

"More people." He got to his feet.

"Where you goin', Matt?"

"Over to Coogan's office. Listen with both ears. Might heap a little more coal on the fire."

"Don't put out the fire."

"I won't."

He crossed the street and entered Coogan's office. "Tough luck," he said.

Mike Endicott, about to leave, had drawn back. Now the rancher stood and looked at the land-locater with hard, probing eyes. The muscles of his mouth were tight.

Chuck Coogan, buckling on his spurs, had one boot on a bench. He let the boot come to the floor, and the spur rowel chimed. Coogan lifted his other leg and said, "Miller worked for you, Wheeler?"

Wheeler looked at the lawman. "I canned him yesterday. I canned him right after he tried to break into Doc's office. Why he tried to break in there is beyond me. He must have been drunk to the point of being loco."

"He wasn't that drunk," Doc Jones said.

Wheeler nodded. "Anyway, I fired him. His actions were beginning to reflect on me, and that wasn't good. Nelson reported that you claimed you lost your blackleg vaccine, Doc Jeff?"

"I didn't *lose* it. Somebody stole it from my office, jimmied the window."

"Who do you suppose stole it?"

Coogan said pointedly, "I'm workin' on the case, Wheeler."

"Is there anything I can do, Deputy?"

Mike Endicott answered that with, "You and your farmers can get off Quarter Circle U grass, Wheeler!"

Wheeler looked sharply at the rancher. "They found a can of kerosene at that fire last night. And it didn't have my name painted on it, Endicott. I had the iron of your Quarter Circle U spread, remember?"

"Somebody stole it off my ranch!" Endicott said strongly.

"That you'll have to prove," Wheeler said. He looked at Coogan. "What do you say, Deputy?"

"What I know," said Coogan, "I keep to myself . . . until the right time comes. What I should do is jail every Quarter Circle U cowboy, including Endicott here, and jug every sodman, too, just for starting that gang fight this morning!"

"My men were merely putting out

a fire started by an arsonist," Wheeler said. "They fought on property owned by one of their members, and they were invaded by the Quarter Circle U cowboys. You can jug the cowpunchers and Endicott, but you'd have a hard time bringing charges against my farmers in a court of law."

Coogan said, "Forget it. Get out, all of you. In the first place, my jail isn't big enough. Only got two cells in it!" The deputy herded them outside and locked his door. "The sheriff might come over and get into this if it gets too tough for one man to handle."

Coogan and Endicott went toward their broncs. Wheeler walked across the street toward his office, his boots making puffs of dust. Doc Jones stood for a moment; then, deciding on a cup of coffee, he went to the Branding Iron Cafe. He really wanted more than a mere cup of java: he wanted to look at a girl named Miss Millicent Simmons. She was in the kitchen, cleaning the stove with a cloth. He came in silently behind her and put both hands on her waist.

She stopped working and looked around at him.

"Oh, it's you, Doc! I thought it was one of my other boy friends."

He let his hands fall. "You only have me for a boy friend, remember?"

She turned, her back against the stove. Her blue eyes glistened.

"You men take too much for granted . . . around a woman."

He put both hands under her elbows. "You'll get too warm next to that stove." He moved her forward and into his arms. She made no move to put her arms around him, but she submitted unresistingly to his embrace, her hands at her sides.

"Aren't you going to fight, Millie?"

"No."

"Why not?"

"You're too big and too strong."

"Aren't you going to put your arms around me?"

"No."

"Why not?"

"I haven't made up my mind yet."

He took a step back and looked down at her with a sudden fear cutting through him, making the angular slopes of his boyish face suddenly pale.

"There's — somebody else?"

"There might be."

Her eyes — blue as rain-washed Montana skied glistened. Her body was not rigid; it melted against him, giving him a strong feeling. Then through the sparkle of her eyes came a shaft of girlish laughter.

"You little devil — You had me scared stiff. You're only faking and . . . "

He kissed her. She kissed him. Her arms were possessingly tight around him. There were only two people in the world. Then, without warning, a third came in, breaking the aura of happiness.

"Could I have some breakfast, Miss Millie?"

Old Man Dial had come in the back door. He had a few wisps of hay hanging to his baggy pants, for evidently he had slept off a drunk in some nearby haymow.

"At this time," said Doc Jones, "you, of all people, have to come in. So it kicked you, eh?"

"With both hind hoofs. Coffee first, Millie, please."

"You're a good advertisement against drinking whiskey," Doc Jones said. "Wish your nose was as sharp as your whiskey appetite."

"I'm sorry, Doc. I got drunk. Otherwise I might have seen the gent what busted into your office. Coffee sure was good, Millie."

"I'll pour more."

Doc Jones said, "Good-bye, you two old drunks."

Doc Jeff went along the alley toward the barn, saddled a fresh horse, and rode down the main street, heading south.

As he rode past Wheeler's office, he glanced through the broken window. Wheeler sat at his desk. Lee Osborne squatted against the wall, his eyes closed — or so it looked to the doc.

Doc Jeff touched spurs to his horse and loped out of town. He rode for about a mile straight south, giving the impression he was heading in that direction and no other; however, about a mile south of Scrub Pine, he suddenly neck-reined his horse to the west and headed straight north. He did not follow the wagon road. He wanted to meet nobody, for he was going to the county seat.

He did not know that Matt Wheeler and Lee Osborne were trailing him. The pair rode on the higher ridges, and they kept back from the foothills. When Doc Jeff veered off the trail, circled the town, and headed north, Wheeler knew he was up to something.

He whistled softly. "Givin' out the idea he was going south, then heading north on a hard lope."

"Where is he a-goin', Matt?"

"County seat, I'd say."

"Why?"

"For two reasons, I think."

"What are they, Matt?"

"Let's trail him."

It was about twenty miles to the county seat, and Doc Jeff pushed his mount hard, lather gathering under the edges of his saddle blanket. When it became apparent that Doc Jeff really was headed for the county seat, Matt Wheeler and Lee Osborne whipped up their mounts and circled around the veterinarian. They were already in town when Doc Jeff single-footed his bronc down the main street.

"What the heck is them two reasons, Matt?"

"First, he might want to talk to the sheriff about the trouble on Scrub Pine. I don't believe he thinks much of Coogan's ability."

"I doubt if he'd go over Coogan like that. That wouldn't be a nice trick to play on Coogan, an' Doc Jeff is honest."

"You got something there. The second reason is that he might wire out for blackleg vaccine."

"He could have wired from Scrub Pine."

"He might want to do it on the quiet, Lee. That way, the vaccine could come in without anybody but himself knowing it had even been ordered. Doc Jeff is a sly one, no two ways around that."

"He sure got that gal away from you."

"What gal?"

"Thet one in the cafe. Millie."

Wheeler smiled. "I like them older. Married once or twice. More experience. He's ridin' into the livery barn now."

The land-locater and his gunman were in a room in a hotel, on the second floor. This county seat, which was named Highring, was about twice the size of Scrub Pine. A railroad branch line ran to Scrub Pine. But, due to lack of freight and passengers, the railroad had almost abandoned it, keeping only an emergency telegraph operator there, who, in addition to running the wire service, also patrolled the track. Rumor held that if and when the farmers raised enough wheat and other produce to ship out, the track would be reopened.

Therefore, the railroad figuratively ended at Highring. From the county seat a stagecoach ran to Scrub Pine every other day. Freight wagons came up once a week with freight and supplies.

Osborne hunkered and squinted out the corner of the window. They had not signed up for this room. They had boldly gone into it after sneaking up the back stairway from the alley. The clerk had not seen them, nor had they signed the register.

Osborne said, "He's leavin' the livery barn. He'd sure be su'prised if he knew we was watchin' him. He figgers we're still in Scrub Pine."

"Keep far enough back," Wheeler warned. He had found a greasy deck of cards in a dresser drawer, and now he played solitaire on the bed. "Keep me posted, Lee," he ordered.

"Sure thing, Matt."

While Wheeler played, Osborne kept up a running chatter. Doc Jeff Jones had just gone into a cafe. Now he came out. He hadn't been in there long. Probably just getting a cup of coffee.

"He's goin' into the depot, Matt."

"He is, eh?"

"You was right," Osborne said. "Bet he aims to wire out for vaccine to be sent in. If the farmers an' Endicott get hold of vaccine, we're through in Scrub Pine, Matt."

Wheeler said, "It's one thing to order it and another gettin' it delivered to Scrub Pine." He glanced at the old alarm clock on the dresser. "He's been in there a little over ten minutes."

"Seems longer to me."

"Always longer when you wait."

Lee Osborne rolled a long wheat-papered cigarette. "What if he orders vaccine, Matt, and it gets to Scrub Pine?"

"Let me worry about that."

11

DOC JEFF JONES sent off two wires. Both went to the territorial capital, which was west in the mountains. One was to a wholesale veterinary house. The other was to the attorney general. The attorney general and Doc Jeff had gone to college together. He was the youngest attorney general the territory had ever had. His boss — a political appointee — had obligingly died right after the young attorney began to work in Helena.

The operator was a dried-up man with sleeve protectors and a green eyeshade. "You want to wait for answers?"

"I do."

The operator studied the messages.

Doc Jeff said, "These are secret, of course. I want not a word about them to get out of this office."

"All messages sent through this office are forgotten as soon as they are sent over the wire."

"Good."

The man went to his key. Doc Jeff took a seat in a far corner. Within a few minutes, a mixed freight-and-passenger train came in. One of the women who got off reminded him somewhat of Millie, and he remembered the sweet push of her young and magnificent body. He sure was lucky!

One of Wheeler's farmers came in and called to the woman. They embraced, then left together. Doc Jeff figured the farmer had not seen him. Evidently, the hoeman had sent East for his wife. Well, she sure would be due for a shock, coming from the civilized East directly into a range war, with cattle dying like flies from blackleg.

Soon Doc Jeff was again the only person in the waiting room. The train departed, showering the platform and depot with hot cinders. The operator cursed the engineer and fireman. Then he swore at the Montana lignite coal used by the locomotive. Doc Jeff was sociable and he agreed with him.

The operator then tried to get information out of the vet. How bad was the trouble over on Scrub Pine? Doc Jeff admitted it was bad. Beyond that, he said nothing; the impression came that this man was a gossip. The operator was persistent. Was it true that the sheriff was sending out special deputies to help Coogan?

"Be a good thing to do," Doc Jeff said.

"Here comes your answer."

The attorney general wired only two words: *I'll investigate*.

Again the operator started his questioning, but Doc Jeff gave him nothing substantial. The key started talking; this time the reply was from the drug-supply company. A carton of blackleg vaccine was being shipped to the Dakotas, but the company would wire ahead, stop the shipment at Great Falls, and have it sent to Highring.

"When will it get here?" Doc Jeff asked.

"Tomorrow, I'd say."

Doc Jeff scowled. "Tomorrow? The mixed train just left. Is there another coming tomorrow?"

There was. Because of the farmers at Scrub Pine, more freight was coming in; therefore, the railroad would run a mixed train each day.

"That land is no good for farming," the operator said. "Them farmers will be starved out, the railroad figures."

Doc Jeff said, "I'm afraid you're right. Wonder how big a supply they sent me?"

"They don't say," the operator said.

Doc Jeff told the man to ship the vaccine to Scrub Pine on the freight wagon, which, by luck, left right after the mixed train arrived.

"Sure will, Doc Jeff."

The vet went outside into the bright sunshine, smiling to himself. He had

had a little luck. Vaccine would reach Scrub Pine tomorrow evening. He and the farmers and Endicott would work hard to try to check this dreadful malady. Doc Jeff had another cup of coffee and then decided to go home. His business here in Highring was over.

To get to the livery barn, he cut through an alley. He was walking behind the Buckhorn Saloon when the sky fell in on him. He had heard the swish of sand on boots, and before he could turn, the blackjack had smashed down on his head. Then the sky turned black, the night roared in, and he dimly remembered starting to fall to the dust.

The next thing he knew, he was trying to sit up. His head felt as if a herd of wild horses were circling his brain. He raised his hands to his eyes, memory rushing back. He had been slugged.

He pulled his hands down. He was sitting on a pool table in a saloon.

He remembered he had been walking behind the Buckhorn Saloon. Evidently, somebody had taken him, unconscious, into the barroom. Men stood around the table.

"Somebody slugged me."

The bartender, a beefy man with hairy arms, said, "We found you in the alley, knocked cold. We toted ye inside. Doc will be over in a minute, they tell me. We take it you're a stranger here in Highring?"

Doc Jeff nodded. He got off the table and, for a moment, thought he would fall. But the big hand of the bartender caught him and held him.

"I can stand — now. And thanks."

Doc Jeff felt of his head. No blood in his hair. Evidently, he had been slugged with a sandbag, or some other instrument that mauled and did not cut.

Suddenly he thought of his telegrams. He had carefully folded them and put them in his shirt pocket. They were still there, carefully folded. He felt of his wallet, usually in his right hip pocket. His wallet, he discovered, was gone. The motive, then, had been robbery only?

"Somebody sure fooled himself," he told the bartender. "If I remember rightly, my purse had a buck and a quarter in it."

The town marshal came with the doctor. Doc Jeff told him his identity. According to the marshal, other citizens had lately been slugged and robbed. He had done his best, but to date . . . He sounded faintly like Deputy Sheriff Chuck Coogan.

"Doc, go easy — that's my head, not yours!"

"You have a mild concussion."

"The word mild," Doc Jeff Jones assured, "is an understatement."

"Get me some water," the doctor said.

The big bartender grinned. "No water in this place, Doc."

A man went outside with an empty whiskey flask. They heard the pump protest. He came in and dumped the water in a glass. The doctor added some powder. It tasted rough, but it helped Doc Jeff's head.

"Thanks," the vet said. "Come up to Scrub Pine some day, Doc, and I'll vaccinate you for blackleg, gratis."

"No money in this job," the doctor said in mock sadness.

"You sound like me in Scrub Pine." Doc Jeff spoke to the bartender. "Give the boys all a shot around; I'll pay you the next time I'm in town."

"On the cuff it goes," the big man said.

A man asked, "Where is your horse, Doc Jeff?" When Jeff told him he said, "I'll lead him back into the alley for you." He added, "Got any *dinero* to pay the livery man?"

"I can't pay him, either."

"He'll take it on credit."

Doc Jeff grinned. "He'll have to . . . or keep my horse."

Within ten minutes, minus his wallet, he was riding out of the county seat, heading for the rim of hills that lay between Highring and Scrub Pine. His head ached, but he had good recuperative powers, for he was young.

Wheeler and Osborne watched him from the upstairs window of the hotel.

"There he goes," Osborne said, "headache and all, headin' for Scrub Pine."

Wheeler played a card. "You slugged him neat, Lee. You sure can handle that blackjack."

"Practice. Sure hope he didn't see me come behind him. He started to turn right afore I lowered the boom on him."

"He never saw you."

"We might have to kill him . . . yet," Lee Osborne said.

"He figures he got slugged for his wallet. He doesn't know we read those telegrams. Now we know about the vaccine coming, and that was what we wanted to know all the time. We outfoxed him."

"For once."

Wheeler looked at Osborne. "We got a ride to make."

They went down the back stairs and into the alley. As they approached their broncs, Wheeler looked back at Highring. "See you tomorrow, maybe," he told the town.

"Why tomorrow?"

"We could check for certain that the vaccine box gets on the freight wagon. Yes, we gotta check that, or we'd stop the freighter for nothing."

"I savvy."

They struck out at a long trail lope that really ate the miles.

Doc Jones did not ride directly to Scrub Pine; he detoured to look at the farmers' cattle. And what he saw did not please him.

Blackleg was rampant on this range. Young cattle were dying. Some were already dead, carcasses bloated and distended, the deadly black sheen on their foreparts. Farmers were desperate. They had anxious, worried faces, and their families were tight groups bound together by a common menace.

"Endicott done brought this in," one farmer said hotly. "He vaccinated his young stuff on the sly during spring calf roundup, and that pertects him while our stock dies."

"He's losing cattle, they tell me."

"I doubt thet! He might say that 'cause he's a liar of the first water, as Matt Wheeler says." Doc Jeff then caught the stink of whiskey on the farmer's breath. "Us farmers oughta git our rifles an' ride over to the Quarter Circle U outfit an' treat it to a little fire!"

Doc Jeff rode on. But each farmer had similar complaints. Wheeler had done good work with his tongue, and the hoemen believed him. Hatred and anger ran high against the Endicott spread. Doc Jeff knew better than to put in a word for Endicott. If he did that, they would accuse him of siding with the rancher.

Doc Jones had lots of work to do.

He ordered the farmers to burn the carcasses of the dead animals. This, he explained, would destroy the germs. Then he rode over to the Endicott Quarter Circle U outfit.

The bull was out on pasture. Stiffness had left his front quarters, and he grazed without pain. Doc Jeff rode to the house. Endicott came out, leaned his rifle against the porch pillar, and said, "Howdy, Doc Jeff."

"Rifle?" Doc Jeff said.

"Thought you was a farmer."

Doc Jeff nodded, dismounting. He ate supper with the Endicotts. Ma Endicott brushed close and whispered, "It worked, Doc Jeff. Oh, he'd be mad if he knew!" Ray's eyes glistened, and he nodded.

Mike Endicott did not hear his wife, nor had he seen his son's nod of affirmation. He was talking with his cowpoke, Jim. Jim had found eight dead yearlings on South Fork.

"Farmers kill them?"

"Blackleg, boss."

Mike Endicott laid down his fork and knife and said, "Darn it, they ain't no blackleg here, even if Doc says so! That bull got better. Somethin' else killed them cattle — either larkspur or loco weed. I'm ridin' out there."

Jim looked at Doc Jones. "Come along, Doc?"

Endicott said, "Doc has rid all day tendin' to the nesters' cattle. Blackleg is wipin' them out, he says. I say it's somethin' else, not blackleg. I'm a good vet myself. I've been doctorin' cattle all my life."

Doc Jeff said, "Got to get to town, Jim. Thanks, though."

Soon the rancher and the cowpuncher thundered out of the yard. Doc Jeff Jones, a few minutes later, thanked Ma Endicott for the good meal and rode toward town. He was tired. The last few days had been hectic, and he longed for a good bed.

He had told nobody about the coming of the vaccine. There was no use in getting these farmers excited.

They had not believed him, just as Endicott still did not believe blackleg was on this grass. He decided they could suffer a few more days.

Wheeler stood to profit. In fact, some of the farmers were already going to town to sell their deeds to Wheeler — if he would buy them. They still trusted Wheeler.

Dusk was thick when Doc Jeff reached Scrub Pine. He ate at the Branding Iron and chatted with Millie, but did not tell her about having ordered the blackleg vaccine. Nor did he tell her about his being slugged and robbed. She did not, in fact, know he had taken the long ride to Highring. Nobody knew that in this town but one man, and his name was Doc Jones.

Wheeler sat on the bench in front of his office, smoking a cigar. When Doc Jeff went by, the land-locater said, "Some of the farmers have been bawlin' on my shoulder. They're losing cattle fast."

"Blackleg."

Wheeler shook his head slowly. "Tough luck. And Endicott claims it's new on this grass, too. Some of my farmers say he vaccinated during spring roundup on the sly, then took in a cow sick with blackleg. Would that spread germs, Doc Jeff?"

"Yes."

Wheeler said, "Gawd, I'm losing the whole thing, Doc Jeff."

The vet studied him momentarily. "What do you mean, Wheeler?"

"You know what I mean. I'm in business here locating homesteaders. That makes me personally responsible for the welfare of my farmers. They're being run out by Endicott. When they leave, my business is shot full of holes."

"They tell me you're buying up homesteads."

"I am."

"Why? — if you don't mind my asking."

"I do mind your asking." Wheeler glanced up at Lee Osborne, who had come out of the office to sit on the bench, too. "But I'll tell you why. I have faith in this country as a farming country. I'm buying these homesteads to eventually farm them myself or resell them. Other farmers will come."

"And you'll rob them, too?"

"Your language, Doc Jeff, is kinda strong."

The vet looked at Lee Osborne. Osborne's eyes were dull, and his lips twitched. Doc Jeff turned his gaze on Wheeler. And the veterinary showed a twisted, ironic little smile.

"We understand each other," he said, and went to his office.

Wheeler regarded the tip of his cigar. "That doc is gettin' too big for his britches. But there's lots of time."

"He talked to the farmers on the way over from Highring," Lee Osborne said. "Them farmers, some of 'em, reported to us. From what I gather, Doc Jeff never told about ridin' over to Highring, nor did he tell about the vaccine coming."

"He's playing his cards close."

Osborne studied his fingers. "He's not so dumb, boss. He might figure that somebody read them telegrams and then refolded them an' tucked them back in his pocket again."

Wheeler blew smoke. "I doubt that."

"We have to consider that angle."

"We sure do. But I doubt if he tells anybody. He wants this to come through in secret. He's smart enough."

"Here comes Coogan."

Wheeler inhaled, then said, "Keep your mouth closed. Say nothing at all unless he asks questions. Let me do the talking."

"I'll go inside."

"No, stay here."

Coogan, a badly dressed and dirty man, slouched up and said, "Nice evenin', gentlemen."

"Sit and rest your bones," Wheeler invited.

"Thanks." But the deputy did not sit on the bench. He went on his hams, his back to the office wall. "When is the new window comin'?"

That was a sore spot with Matt Wheeler. "A few days, they tell me."

"Same sign painted on the new one?"

Was this dumb deputy deliberately rubbing his fur the wrong way? "Same sign," Matt Wheeler said, and stiffness crept in despite his efforts.

Coogan dug and came out with a pipe. He dug again and came out with a tobacco pouch. The match flare showed his wide and whiskery face.

"Cattle," he said, "cattle . . . "

Wheeler waited, as did Lee Osborne.

"Cattle dying. Dying like proverbial flies. All the farmers are losing stock. So is Endicott."

"I doubt that latter."

"He told me. South Fork, they died."

"Blackleg?"

"He claims not. He's too darned stubborn to admit it. He's a hard-shelled one, Mike is. Cowpuncher I talked to said they had died of blackleg. Just saw him down in the Merc."

"They tell me Endicott vaccinated his young stuff. Did it on the sly during spring calf roundup."

"Who told you that, Wheeler?"

"One of Endicott's riders. Fellow just hired for spring roundup. Told me that here in town last spring, but I paid it no attention. Just happened to recall it now. The fellow left this section."

"Which fellow was that?"

Wheeler hurriedly thought back. Who had worked the spring roundup for the Quarter Circle U and then had been laid off the Endicott payroll? Finally, a name came to him.

"August Smith."

"I remember him. Hired as a circle rider. So he told you that, eh? Endicott told me that was a lie circulated by the farmers."

"Endicott has his back to the wall."

Deputy Sheriff Coogan stood up, pipe making sounds as he sucked. "We all got our backs to the wall, Wheeler. You'll lose your farmers, and the farmers'll lose their cattle, and

Endicott, if blackleg hits his outfit, will go broke. There's only one hope, and it will come late maybe — too late. Before it comes about, there'll be lots of dead cattle."

"And that — hope?"

"That Doc Jeff gets some vaccine in. He can't save them cows that are dead or those that have gone too far, but he can save some of the young stuff that ain't developed too much sickness yet."

"Has he ordered any?" Lee Osborne asked.

"I dunno. I hope so. Be some days 'til it gits here, though. And lots of cattle can die in the meantime."

"Wonder who stole the vaccine out of his office?" Wheeler wanted to know.

"Me, I could find no clues."

Osborne said slowly, "I hate to say this, but maybe Endicott or one of his men lifted that vaccine to keep the farmers from getting it."

"That sounds loco," Coogan snarled.

Osborne spread his hands. "Okay,

okay, stay cool under the collar, Coogan. Just a idea, nothing more."

Coogan scowled, and sucked his pipe. The idea, Osborne saw, had been planted. But would it sprout and bear fruit?

"Just an idea," Osborne repeated.

Coogan said, "Gotta make my rounds."

He moved off into the dusk, a man bent with the demands of his job. Osborne looked at Matt Wheeler. "How was that, Matt?"

"Good!"

"For onct I did somethin' right, eh?"

"One more thing, Lee. Check on the vet. Watch him until he hits the hay. He might try to pull a fast one on us."

12

DOC JONES did not sleep well. He awoke toward midnight, remembering how he had been slugged in Highring. He was out of bed early. After a modest breakfast, he went to the livery barn and got his bronc.

Lee Osborne, at that moment, was shaking his boss awake. "The doc — he's left town, Matt. Wake up, darn it!"

Wheeler rolled over, instantly awake. "Where did he go, Lee?"

"Rode north toward Highring."

Wheeler was already dressing. He pulled on his boots. "He might be going over to check on that vaccine to see that it gets here safe. Did he take a pack horse with him?"

"No, and why ask that — ?"

"That vaccine will come in a big box, I suppose. Packed in a lot of sawdust or shavings to keep it from being broke. I figure he might aim to tote it out himself."

"He jus' rid out on a saddle bronc, Matt."

Wheeler buckled on his spurs, "Get our horses. I'll meet you in the alley. Where is your rifle?"

"In the corner there, with yours."

"Take it with you. Get some cartridges out of the drawer. This might call for Winchester work, Lee. Long-range work."

Osborne picked up his rifle. "You carry some cartridges. I'll get the broncs. So this might be the last day that Doc Jeff is alive, eh?"

"It might be if he tries to get that vaccine through."

Wheeler went to the rack and got his Winchester .30-30. He broke the breech, saw the dull rim of the cartridge in the barrel, and slammed shut the mechanism, easing the hammer down to safety position. Then, from the desk drawer, he took out two boxes of cartridges and was ready to ride.

Doc Jones headed for the Endicott spread. On the way, he stopped at the home of a farmer; the man had three dead yearlings, and two more were down, victims of blackleg. He implored Doc Jeff to get some blackleg vaccine. Doc Jeff thought he would have vaccine within a few days, maybe longer — he wanted to make no definite commitments. At this information, the farmer almost cried; by that time, his cattle would be dead.

"Some of you farmers wouldn't let me vaccinate when I had the vaccine to do it with," Doc Jeff reminded him.

"Not me. You kin shoot all the germs you want into my stock if it pulls them through. Heck, I'm busted. I gotta sell out and drift. Wonder if Endicott will buy my deed?"

"He might. I'm going over that way."

The farmer rode with Doc Jeff. As they neared the Quarter Circle U, the man got very nervous.

"I'm afraid of Endicott."

Endicott wouldn't listen to the man. The man said he would sell to Wheeler. Endicott got mad. Sell to Wheeler, he said, and then he, Endicott, would run out Matt Wheeler. The farmer loped away, also angry. And Doc Jeff looked at the rancher and shook his head.

"What t'heck is wrong with you, hoss doctor?"

"There was a chance to get a deed cheap. Now it'll go to Wheeler."

"Let it go. Nobody can farm that land. Wheeler will go broke trying." The rancher scowled. "Wheeler knows that land is no good, that there is so danged little rain that crops won't grow. What's behin' his wantin' that land, Doc Jeff?"

"I don't know. How is the bull?"

"Perfectly well."

They went to the corral and looked at the bull. No swelling in his shoulders, and his skin was losing its black tinge and becoming cream-colored again.

"He's all well," Doc Jeff said.

"He didn't have blackleg."

Young Ray had come upon the scene. Clara Endicott watched through the window of the kitchen. She was frowning as she cooked breakfast. for once, young Ray was not talkative.

"This boy ain't well," Mike Endicott said. "Last day or so he's moped around, and he don't talk. Usually he talks the leg off'n everybody he meets, Doc. Why don't you look at him?"

"He's all right."

"I'm not sick," Ray said stoutly.

Doc Jones petted the bull and did not look at Mike Endicott when he asked, "You losin' any other young stock, Mike?"

"Yeah, I've lost some."

"Many?"

Endicott lied. "Not many."

"What are the symptoms?"

"Jes' like this bull here. Get stiff shoulders. I lay it onto the fact thet they bed down on the danged hard ground. Just like concrete, it is — drought has hung on so long."

Jeff nodded, saying nothing.

Ma Endicott came out, wiping her hands on her apron. "Mike and Ray, come in for breakfast. Have you eaten yet, Doc Jeff?"

Doc Jeff smiled. "That's why I came out here," he admitted with a grin.

"Come on in an' set," Mike Endicott said gruffly.

This was a real breakfast: eggs, toast, bacon, mush, and plenty of coffee, good coffee. A breakfast like this, he realized, even made marriage worthwhile. This thought brought Millie Simmons to mind. She could cook, too.

He decided to needle Mike Endicott a little.

"Farmers maintain, Mike, that you vaccinated against blackleg when you had spring roundup, and then you put blackleg on this grass to get rid of them."

"They what?" The rancher almost exploded. His cheeks puffed out and became blue, and he spewed coffee. "Do they really say that, Doc Jeff?"

"They sure do. I don't want to make you mad, but when I talked with that farmer this morning, he claimed one of your spring roundup riders — August Smith — told that to somebody, I don't know who."

"Smith? He's gone! I only hired him for spring roundup. He drifted on right after I paid him."

"He might've drifted, but he was supposed to say that before he left."

"He lied! If I get my hands on him . . ."

Ma Endicott said, "Dad, you're almost stuttering, you're so mad. Remember your heart, please." She winked at Doc Jeff. Her husband did not see the wink, but Ray did.

"Nothin' wrong with my heart, woman! That's a lie — a bald-faced, unmitigated lie, it is!"

"The farmers don't think so. You aren't losing any cattle to blackleg, and that looks suspicious to them."

Doc Jeff knew he had the rancher cornered. Endicott had to either admit

201

losing cattle to blackleg or say he had vaccinated.

"Looks suspicious to them," Doc Jeff repeated.

But Endicott only said, "T'heck with them and Wheeler and Osborne." And he would say no more.

Doc Jeff thanked Mrs. Endicott and pushed back his chair. He felt a little defeated, for he had wanted to break through to Mike Endicott, and he had not done this. Endicott dug into his mush with apparent dissatisfaction.

"Will you look at Ray's saddle horse, Doc Jeff?" Ma asked.

"Sure."

Ray followed his mother and Doc Jeff to the barn. Once inside, the woman said, "I'm afraid to tell him about vaccinating that bull. He'll go hog-wild, he has such a temper."

"We're in a mess," Ray said, his young face worried.

"Are you losing cattle to blackleg?"

Ma Endicott was really worried. Quarter Circle U cattle, young stock, were dying out on the range, and still her husband would not bend his will. They were facing ruin. After a quarter of a century of hard work, they were facing bankruptcy, and her husband would not admit it.

"It would do no good, anyway," Doc Jeff said. "I have no vaccine. I'm getting some, but I don't know when it will come. Without vaccine, I'm harmless to save cattle. The farmers have their own ideas as to who broke into my office and stole my vaccine."

"What is that?" the woman asked.

Doc Jeff debated a moment, then decided to tell her. "They say that Mike had somebody break into my office and steal the vaccine to keep it from reaching them and their cattle. They say he does not need vaccine because, like I said, they claim he vaccinated on the sly during spring roundup."

"They say that?"

"They do, Mrs. Endicott."

"They lie," Ray said hotly.

"I figure they do," Doc Jeff said. "But they don't know Mike as I do. To them, Mike and his outfit are a menace."

Ma Endicott's wide face was pale. "This might mean range war, Doc Jeff! Our hands have already fought the farmers in a fist-fight, but this time they might storm our ranch with rifles!"

Doc Jeff said, "Anything can happen."

"Wheeler and his gunmen are behind this," Ray said angrily. "They want the farmers to fight Dad, and they'll win by sitting to one side. Dad said that yesterday, he did. I heard him."

"Maybe I should tell him we vaccinated the bull, Doc Jeff?"

"Do what you think best, Mrs. Endicott."

Doc Jeff mounted and rode away, leaving the mother and son standing in front of the barn. Maybe it would have been best to have let the bull die, he thought sardonically. Then Endicott would have had to admit that blackleg

204

was on Quarter Circle U grass. But it would have been tough on the bull. And the bull, after all, was what had counted.

He realized he was fighting blackleg germs. Besides, he was fighting ignorance, pride, and bigotry. He kept remembering the tragic eyes of the farmer he had met that morning. He remembered the worried look in Mike Endicott's eyes, for the man was losing his empire to an invisible germ. Endicott's look had been the same as that which had haunted the farmer's tragedy-stricken eyes. Doc Jones had only two hopes. One, that the vaccine would arrive on time; the other, that the attorney general would send out territorial officers to force the farmers to vaccinate their cattle.

He stopped at Terry Brendan's homestead. When he rode in the yard, he saw that the rancher's cattle were down. One carcass lay bloated and ugly in the pasture. The rancher's face was wild, and he carried his rifle.

"Figured mebbe you were a Endicott rider snoopin' aroun', Doc."

"You know how to shoot that rifle?"

"I'm practicin'."

Doc Jones said, "You talk and act like a fool, Brendan. That dead cow — burn her carcass to kill the germs. Your other stock — that young stuff that is down — all have blackleg."

"You don't need to tell me. I know!"

"If you'd have let me vaccinate, those cattle would have been all right now."

Brendan's wife had come to the door. Her eyes were red from crying.

"When you get vaccine, Doc Jeff, you can sure vaccinate any of our stock any time you want to," the woman said.

Brendan whirled on her and snarled, "Go back in the house. I'm the boss here. No cow of mine will get germs shot into her, savvy?"

"He'll vaccinate, even if I have to stand over you with a rifle, Terry."

Brendan looked at Doc Jeff. His

sunken face, haggard and tired, held conflict.

Doc Jeff leaned from his saddle. "It might not be up to you to call the hand, Brendan. I've called the territorial health officials in on this. If they want to vaccinate your cattle, they'll vaccinate whether you like it or not. Or else you'll go to jail."

"I'll go to jail first."

Doc Jeff looked at Mrs. Brendan. "I admire him for his stand," he said, "but I feel sorry for him because of his bullheadedness. Good day, madam."

All of the farmers had cattle either dead or down. Anger was strong against the Endicott spread. Most of the farmers still showed black-and-blue marks from the fight at the burning cabin.

Doc Jeff listened, said little, and did some more thinking. Then, about ten o'clock, he headed across country for Highring to check on the arrival of his vaccine. Lee Osborne and Matt Wheeler were already in Highring, in the same hotel that they sneaked into the day before.

"Cleaned it since yesterday," Osborne said. "Swept up the cigar butts."

Wheeler thumbed the deck of cards. "Bet they wonder who was in here. Well, I'm going to beat this game or know the reason why."

Osborne watched, crouched by the window. He kept reporting back to Matt Wheeler. Doc Jones had gone to the depot. He and the agent were looking at a big box on the depot platform.

"How big is it, Lee?"

"Purty big."

"Give me some dimensions."

"Oh, about three by two feet, something like that. Too big to pack on a saddle bronc."

"Good."

"They're puttin' it on the freight wagon now, boss."

Wheeler moved over, cards in hand, and squinted. "Toward the back, and on top. Which is just right for us. A man could come in behind that load and nobody would see him climb up and take down that box, what with that bunch of boxes high between him and the driver."

"Driver'd never see him even if he looked back. Load is too high right behind his seat."

Wheeler returned to his game. "Good."

"That wagon is almost ready to move, Matt. There goes Doc Jones back to his horse. He's ridin' out of town."

"Follow him, Osborne."

Lee Osborne studied his boss. "Why?"

Matt Wheeler spoke roughly. "He's no fool, that vet. He's wise; he's showed it today. He figures somebody read them telegrams and put them back in his pocket. He's so wise he won't follow the wagon directly or ride with the driver. Follow him, Osborne."

"He'll ride the ridges, you mean?"

"Yes, and watch that wagon."

Osborne wet his lips, and nodded.

"You got somethin' there, Matt."

Wheeler said slowly, "Follow him . . . and kill him."

"Kill him?"

"Yes, in the badlands. Winchester work, at long range. Then, when I hear the shooting, or when you give me a signal, I'll get this stuff off the wagon. The driver will never miss it until he gets to Scrub Pine."

"I'll kill him, Matt — with pleasure."

Wheeler gripped his gunman's shoulder hard. "A clear head, a steady eye, and this vet is gone for good. Now get out of here — and don't miss."

"I won't."

Lee Osborne went down the back stairs. Wheeler moved to the window. The freight wagon was rolling out of Highring; Wheeler watched for a moment. Then he heard steps outside in the hall. He moved to the wall and flattened himself beside the door, rifle barrel raised.

Outside, a man talked to himself.

"Gent went down the back. Strange fellow. Came from upstairs. Yesterday, a room dirty — not rented."

The door opened. A head, fringed with short hair and bald as a billiard ball in its center, stuck itself into the room. The owner of the head did not see Matt Wheeler. Nor did he see the fall of the Winchester's barrel.

The barrel hit the man behind the head, pulling him forward into the room. He crashed into a chair, rolled over, and lay still.

Wheeler said, "He'll never know who or what hit him!" He grinned, lips pulled back, then wiped his Winchester's barrel on the man's shirt. The man's chest rose and fell. He looked happy, for he had a foolish smile on his whiskery mouth.

Wheeler said, "Sleep and dream, Grandpa."

Then he went downstairs to the alley, mounted, and rode out of Highring, smiling to himself.

13

UNKNOWN to Doc Jones, he had been outmaneuvered by Matt Wheeler. After the vet had ridden out of the county seat, he had taken to the high country, just as Wheeler had instructed.

Doc Jeff was not sure whether anyone had read the two telegrams in his pocket. But it seemed odd that anybody would slug him, in broad daylight, just for the contents of the wallet. He had displayed no great sums of money in public. According to the town marshal, the other victims who had been slugged in Highring had been pretty drunk and had flashed big wads of money around saloons and gambling dens.

This information had made the vet do some thinking. Maybe the person who had slugged him had trailed him into Highring, scouted his movements, and knocked him out to read the telegrams. And this person had then stolen his wallet just to make him believe the motive had been robbery alone.

That was probable and possible.

He had first thought to ride out on the freight wagon. But logic had dispelled this theory. Both he and the driver would be sitting ducks for any holdup men. He would ride guard on the vaccine, but from a distance.

Accordingly, after leaving Highring, he went into the hills, intending to ride to the west side of the wagon trail. His intention was to ride the ridges, watching the wagon all the time, and if a holdup threatened, to ride down and break it up. He hoped his suspicions were wrong. But he had to be sure. The fate of hundreds of head of cattle depended on that vaccine getting to Scrub Pine.

He saw the wagon leave town and inch up the grade. He sat his bronc in some pine trees and watched. He had his Winchester across the fork of his saddle. The wagon, heavily laden, climbed the grade slowly. It reached the summit, and its speed increased slightly as it went down to Wildwood Creek. Then it moved ponderously across the wooden bridge and again started to climb, teams pulling against their collars.

The sun rose, gathered heat, then started to fall. But heat hung across this wilderness, sucking moisture out of plants and the soil. The wagon moved, and Jeff Jones moved with it, keeping hidden as much as possible. When the wagon was about five miles from Scrub Pine, he glimpsed a rider on a hill across the gully, the wagon trail between the rider and himself.

The rider moved across a clearing, then became lost from view. And Doc Jeff frowned. The rider — too distant to recognize — was apparently scouting the wagon, too.

The thought came that perhaps he had glimpsed a Quarter Circle U rider.

One of the farmers had said that the Endicott men were riding night and day during this crisis. They were moving across Quarter Circle U grass. Ahead of the wagon was Endicott Grade, a long slant about two miles in length. Once on top of the grade, the wagon would have it downhill into Scrub Pine.

The rider had apparently gone into the high brush. Jones, sitting his horse on a ridge, suddenly looked to the north. There was a high lift of timber, and he had glimpsed something there.

He jumped from his saddle and hit the ground. At that moment, a rifle, up there on the ridge, popped with savage ferocity. The bullet, meant for Doc Jeff, went low, hitting the horse. It killed the animal instantly. The bronc, before falling, had lunged ahead, dead on his hoofs, the movement perfectly involuntary. Doc Jeff, who had stumbled, rolled to one side, rifle raised, and this quick movement kept the horse from crushing him. The vet, though, was dazed from his fall.

Another rifle bullet, coming in hard and swift, smashed into the gravel, then ricocheted across space. The bullet landed behind Doc Jeff, who was running wildly for the brush, crouched over his rifle. They had outfoxed him, whoever they were!

Two riders, then. One across the canyon, the other on the ridge. And he was on foot now, his bronc dead!

Lee Osborne, hunkered up there on the slope, had missed twice and was angry. But he knew why he had missed. Despite Matt Wheeler's orders, Osborne had rolled a forbidden marijuana cigarette. And the cigarette, working on the pupils of his eyes, had distorted his vision. Otherwise he probably would have ambushed and killed Doc Jones.

Osborne swore methodically. Rifle raised, he waited and watched.

Cheek pressing the battered stock, he shot again. His bullet came closer than he had figured, for he had shot blind into the brush that hid Doc Jones, who lay on his belly, somewhat stunned by his fall.

Jones, gathering his legs under him, suddenly ran for higher brush. He could not see the freight wagon now, for he was in a shallow depression, the bottom of which was dense with buckbrush.

Had the wagon driver heard the shooting? Probably. But he might think it was only a farmer out shooting a deer.

Doc Jeff, on one knee, fired three times. His bullets drew a return fire. There remained only one thing to do. He would work his way high on the slope and get at a position over the ambusher, whoever the ambusher was.

But this task was a hard one. And the ambusher might also have the same idea. Doc Jeff halted, frowning, studying the ridge. It was a waste of bullets to fire blind again into that buckbrush. Next time he let his hammer fall, he would have the ambusher in the sights. Or he would fire at the smoke left by the man's rifle.

Up on the ridge, Lee Osborne was shaking like an old man with ague. Marijuana had thrown his bullets wide. If Matt Wheeler knew about it, he would kill him.

He had to get out fast. Once, he had had courage; dope had sapped him, left him a coward. He had to retreat.

Also, Doc Jeff Jones's bullets, although fired by mere guesswork, had come very close. Lee Osborne had a streak of blood on his left cheek where a sliver of rock had cut him. At first, Osborne had thought a bullet had hit him. And, at that moment, the thought of death drove through him.

Bent over his rifle, he ran unseen over the ridge, glad that boulders covered his retreat. He grabbed his reins, went hurriedly into his saddle, and rode down the canyon, following a dim trail.

The sound of his bronc's hoofs drifted back to Doc Jones. He crouched, rifle raised a little; he cocked his head and listened. Over the ridge ran a horse with wild speed. Had the ambusher lost his courage? Was he pulling stakes? Or was this a trick to get him out into the open?

The thought came that maybe the ambusher had tied reins over the saddle horn, then quirted his bronc across the rump to make him run with an empty saddle.

He decided not to expose himself if he could help it. He worked forward and upward, still hoping to get altitude. He had watched his back trail on the ride out from Highring. He had seen no rider tailing him. This ambusher was no new hand at this game.

Finally, after about twenty minutes — the longest twenty minutes he had ever lived — the veterinarian gained the summit. He had drawn no fire and could see no ambusher below him.

Far in the distance was a rider — dim against the ridge, a dot against space.

Maybe a Quarter Circle U cowboy? Maybe a farmer? Or maybe the ambusher?

He looked at the freight wagon. It was just topping the last grade. It was within about fifty feet of the summit and about half a mile away. Slowly it went upward. Apparently, it had not been halted. Or had it?

He decided the wagon had not been stopped. Had it been halted, it would not have been so close to the summit. He looked at the wilderness beyond the wagon. No sign of the rider.

The thought came that he was on foot. He hollered and waved his shirt, hoping to catch the driver's attention, but if the man saw and heard him, he did not wave back; soon he would be out of sight over the ridge, going down to Scrub Pine town.

An hour later, he hiked into the homestead of Millie's uncle, Clay Simmons. There was a little water in Clear Creek. He drank and then doused his head in the waterhole.

Clay Simmons was a short, middle-aged man. "What the heck, Doc? Where's your bronc?"

"Fell with me back in the hills. Broke both front legs, so I shot him. Gave me quite a fall in the brush. Can I borrow a horse from you, Clay?"

"I ain't got much in the line of a ridin' horse, Doc Jeff. There's that old sorrel work mare there under the trees trying to keep cool. Slap a saddle on her and return her when you can."

The old mare was well broken. Doc Jeff walked up to her and put the bridle on her.

"You got any losses to blackleg, Clay?"

"Not a one, Doc Jeff. So far, that is; it can hit anytime, though, eh?"

"If there are germs on your grass, yes."

Clay Simmons chewed tobacco. He was a bachelor, and had raised Millicent after her folks were killed in a team runaway.

"Odd thing," Clay said slowly.

"Them farmers what are situated on the worst sections of land are hit the hardest, they tell me. I'm kinda alone up here on Clear Creek, so mebbe that is why my stock ain't got it. When will you get some vaccine, Doc?"

Doc Jeff debated. This man was Millie's uncle, and he knew how he and Millie regarded each other, so there was no danger in telling him about the vaccine. By this time, the vaccine should be safe in town, anyway.

"I got some coming in on the freight wagon today. Should be in town now. Keep it to yourself, though."

"Why the secrecy?"

"I have to dole it out to each farmer. I can't afford to let each farmer get all he wants, because I couldn't get that much from the wholesale house."

"Me, I'm a clam, Doc Jeff. Doc, when you hook up with that niece of mine, make her take care of me, eh? I haven't had a good meal for months. Not since she started that highfalutin' eatin' palace down in town."

Doc Jeff swung up. "Maybe she won't have me."

"Don't joke yourself, Doc. The minute she seen you, she figured to hook you. Take care of yourself."

Doc Jeff reined the old mare around. "How about these farmers, Clay? They really hot against the Endicott spread?"

The bachelor showed a studious, thoughtful face. "They claim Endicott has vaccinated on the quiet and took blackleg in. Thet land-locater and his sidekick are behind most of the talk."

"What's behind all this, Clay?"

"Land. That land-locater wants the farmers to move; then he'll own their deeds. Or so it looks to me."

"But the land — it isn't worth having just for cattle, is it? It's the worst part of Endicott's graze."

"So it looks to me, too."

Doc Jeff said, "Keep your ears pinned back and your mouth closed. Hope this old plug can get me into town."

"She'll haul you there, but she's slow."

The mare was slow — very slow. She had three gaits, Doc Jeff thought wryly: walk, stumble, and fall down. He found nine head of Quarter Circle U cattle dead on Down Creek. When Endicott said he was losing no cattle to blackleg, he was fooling no one, including himself. All of these yearlings had died from blackleg. On his ride into Scrub Pine, Doc Jeff Jones saw other dead Quarter Circle U cattle, all victims of blackleg. A sort of anger arose in him, directed toward the bullheaded Mike Endicott. Or was he just bullheaded? Maybe he was lacking in intelligence, too?

By now, Doc Jeff was sure that either Matt Wheeler or Lee Osborne had tried to kill him. He and his professional skill were what stood between Wheeler and his absolute control of Scrub Pine grass. Wheeler might have trailed him to Highring, have slugged him, then read the messages, restoring them to his pocket again. This was logical, but he could not prove it.

He stopped at Barclay's farm.

"How come you ride thet ol' hoss of Clay's?" the man asked.

"My business."

"Mister, you sure sound tough, eh?"

Barclay had the smell of whiskey around him.

"Losing any cattle?" Doc Jeff asked.

"My whole bunch of young stuff is down, all seven of them. Two about ready to die. And they tell me that Endicott hasn't lost a head of stock. Even that bull you said had blackleg — he got well without bein' vaccinated. Us farmers might ride against the Quarter Circle U an' wipe the spread out with fire — just like Endicott or his hired hands fired thet cabin t'other night."

"You're drunk," Doc Jeff said, turning the old mare.

Barclay reached out and grabbed the reins, holding the old horse steady. "Doc, I'm not drunk. You're workin' for Endicott, eh? Mebbe he had you plant this blackleg on this grass?"

"You're still drunk."

"All the time you stick up for Endicott." The farmer glared up at Doc Jones with wicked, bloodshot eyes. "He payin' you to git us farmers out, Doc Jones?"

"Drunk again," Doc Jeff said. "I want no trouble, Barclay."

"What you git in this world an' what you want is two different things. Some claim you murdered that pore George Miller."

"Close your big mouth, or I'll close it!"

"You talk big, Doc, but you bite small. Some of the farmers claim you never had thet vaccine stole outa your office. They claim you said somebody stole it to make it look like you lost it, and all the while you'd taken it to Endicott's outerfit to doctor his cows, jes' cause he's got more money than us pore ones. What about that, Doc?"

"You been out riding range, Barclay?"

"No. Why ask that?"

"Endicott is losing young stuff. His

grass is dotted with carcasses. If I smuggled the vaccine to him, how come his cattle still die?"

"I think you lie — I know you lie!"

Doc Jeff held back his anger with difficulty. Then he decided this man was not worth anger; whiskey was talking, not the man.

Unexpectedly, he placed his boot against the farmer's shoulder. Before Barclay knew what had happened, he was down in the dust. And Doc Jones was riding away.

He met Nelson, who was riding range. The farmer's face was gaunt, and dust was thick on him. His black eyes glistened.

"My cattle," the Norwegian said. "Dyin', or dead. Doc Jeff, we gotta git vaccine, do you hear me?"

"Getting it in as fast as I can."

"Endicott — he stole that vaccine from your office! He used it himself, and he let our cattle die. We meet tonight — all of us — at Brendan's farm. With rifles, too. This thing has to end, like Wheeler says."

Doc Jeff Jones shrugged. "You fools wanta get killed, it's all right with me."

"Don't tell no cowmen about the meetin'. Reckon I shouldn't have told you, seein' you an' Endicott is such friends."

"You don't have to worry, Nelson. The minute you men start toward Brendan's, Mike Endicott will know. He's not so dumb he hasn't scouts out. And when you ride for war with the Quarter Circle U, Endicott will know you're coming!" Doc Jeff showed a tight smile.

Within ten minutes or so, he had reached Scrub Pine. The loaded freight wagon stood in front of the Branding Iron Cafe, and Old Man Dial sat on the sidewalk, a beer bottle beside him.

Doc Jeff went into the cafe. The driver was eating at the counter. Millie was in the kitchen, evidently, for the vet heard the rattle of pots back there. He took a stool beside the driver.

"You got a box for me — on your load?"

"I sure have, Doc Jeff. Big one, too, on the back of the load. Behind that big box there for the Mercantile."

"I'll get it."

Doc Jeff went outside and climbed up on the load. He looked at labels, but found none with his name. Panic started to grow in him. He jumped down and hurried into the restaurant.

"There's no box there with my name on it. And it left Highring, I'm sure. I saw it loaded."

The driver looked at him. "Then if it was loaded in Highring, it is still there. Here is my manifesto." He threw the book on the table and his forefinger found *Doc Jeff Jones, Scrub Pine, Montana Territory*. "On the back of the load, Doc Jeff. Never stopped anywhere but to rest my hosses. Never was off'n the seat at any time. Never even stopped to talk with nobody. Gotta be there."

Doc Jeff went back again and looked,

but did not find the box. The driver, worried now, also left the cafe, coffee cup in hand.

Doc Jones said, "The depot agent and I loaded it down in Highring. That box isn't on that load now. You haven't moved cargo any since leaving Highring, have you?"

"You helped load it? In Highring?"

"You weren't at your load yet. You were eating at the cafe, or something. I cut across country to Scrub Pine."

The driver scowled. "That's right. Depot agent mentioned you, said to be careful of that box. That's why it rode on top, to get no weight on it. The box has to be there."

The driver hurriedly climbed onto the load and looked over the labels. He straightened, scowling in puzzlement.

"Was right here," he said, pointing.

Millie had come out of the cafe. Her hand went into Doc Jeff's. "What's the matter?" she asked.

Doc Jeff said, "Lost a box, honey."

The driver went over his load and

got on the seat. Sitting there, he looked back; he could not have seen the box because of the big carton of goods bound for the Mercantile.

The driver stood up, swearing under his breath. "That box must've fell off, Doc Jeff."

"We had it tied down. The guy ropes are still tied, but there's slack in them — as if the box had been slid out from under them without untying the rope."

The driver nodded. "Or else somebody could have run in behind the wagon, back on one of them grades where the teams are slowed down to a walk, and climbed on the load without me seein' them, lifted thet box, an' dropped off the back again, stealin' it."

Doc Jeff nodded.

Millie asked, "What was in the box, Doc Jeff?"

From across the street came Lee Osborne and Matt Wheeler. Doc Jeff noticed, idly, that Osborne had a slight cut on his cheek.

Again Millie asked, "What was in it, Doc Jeff?"

Wheeler cut in with, "What's wrong here, men?"

The driver answered. "We lost a carton on the way out from Highring, Wheeler. Belonged to Doc Jeff here."

Doc Jeff looked at Millie. "It contained blackleg vaccine," he said.

14

THE Quarter Circle U rider almost killed his bronc in getting to the home ranch from Scrub Pine town. He came into the yard on a lathered cayuse and reined in, dust flying.

"Mike! Oh, Mike!"

Endicott came out of the office, a log building situated between the main house and the bunkhouse. He carried a ledger in his hand, and a pencil was in his mouth.

"What's the matter with you, Jim?" His words were indistinct because of the pencil, so he spat it out. "Why kill good hossflesh in this heat? Are you drunk, cowboy?"

"Never soberer in my life. Mike, there's trouble, and it's comin' our way, right pronto!"

"More blackleg?"

"No — the farmers."

Mike Endicott said, "I got enough troubles without thinkin' of them hoemen. My cattle are dyin' like flies."

Jim had dismounted. The old mozo hobbled over for the cowboy's bronc.

"Doc Jeff Jones got some vaccine sent to Highring. A big box of it, he says. On the way out on the freight wagon, somebody come in behind without the driver seeing him an' stole that box of vaccine!"

"My Gawd! Who stole it — one of the farmers?"

The discussion had brought Ma Endicott and Ray out of the house and cowpunchers from the bunk-house. Even the old mozo, holding the reins of Jim's bronc, listened.

"Nobody knows. They backtracked toward Highring, thinkin' mebbe the box had slipped off, but they didn't find it. But that ain't all, Mike. Them farmers blame the robbery on us Quarter Circle U men!"

"They're loco. We never stole thet vaccine, and we can whip the man thet says my outerfit lifted it!"

"That's prob'ly what we'll have to do," Jim said, his face serious. "And I'm not joking, either. These farmers are being fed lies by Wheeler and Osborne. First we're blamed for thet fire the other night when the farmer's shack burned down. Then they claim we busted into Doc Jeff's office an' stole thet vaccine. Now they claim we stole this vaccine to keep it from gettin' to their cattle. Some even claim we planted blackleg germs on this grass."

"But our cattle would die if we did that. Don't make sense — "

"Oh, yes, it does, Mike. They claim we vaccinated on the sly during spring roundup. Wheeler and Osborne claim one of our men told them that — one of them drifters you hired jes' for spring roundup."

"I'll kill Wheeler, an' Osborne, too."

Ma Endicott cut in with, "Oh, no,

Mr. Mike Endicott. You don't match guns with Wheeler or Osborne, alone or together!"

"Keep your mouth outa this, Ma!"

"I won't, Mr. Endicott. You've played every card wrong, and you know it. Blackleg is eating up your young cattle, and you're so stubborn you won't admit it."

"Them farmers must be stupid," the cowman growled. "Cain't they see dead Quarter Circle U cows almost every place they look, Jim?"

Jim shook his head. "They don't ride the range, Mike. They stay close to their shacks for fear we might try to burn them down. They get fed propaganda by Wheeler and Osborne, and they believe it all."

"Some of 'em don't," Ma Endicott said. "They all can't be that dumb, I'm sure. Doc Jeff Jones will try to talk some sense into them."

Mike Endicott snorted. "Doc Jeff Jones! Heck of a vet he is — can't even diagnose a case of blackleg. If'n thet bull would have had blackleg, he'd a been dead afore now by a day or so. Doc is no good, I tell you."

"Oh, you talk like a complete idiot, Mike Endicott!"

Ma went to the house, Ray following her.

"Ma, we gotta tell him," Ray said.

"I guess you're right, Son."

"He'll bust a cylinder, but we gotta tell him."

"First opportune time, Ray."

Mike and his men kept on talking, a tight knot in the dusk. Scouts drifted in and out. Mike went to his office, put his boots on his desk, and glowered at them. He did not light a lamp.

A rider came in and said, "Boss, the farmers are headin' toward Brendan's farm. They're leavin' their women an' kids home on guard, an' they're ridin' over to Brendan's."

"Meetin' of war, eh?"

"Reckon so, boss."

"We oughta ride over there an' wipe

them out, Scott."

Scott chewed tobacco slowly. "You're the boss," he said at length. "I kinda hate to remind you of this, Mike, but us boys ain't pullin' down gunfightin' wages. We're drawin' cowpuncher wages."

"You boys afraid of them farmers?"

"No, we jes' don't hate a one of 'em, boss. They ain't behin' this, nohow — thet land-locater is. Ma done give us orders not to fight unless them farmers attack us. Ma says — "

"Since when did Ma start givin' orders on this spread?"

"She's run it for years, only you never knew it." The cowpuncher grinned. "Mike, there must be some way short of outright war. Them men has families, an' some of them — an' us too — will git kilt."

"Get the heck out, Scott!"

Scott stopped at the door. He knew his boss better than Mike knew himself. Scott spat on the floor. A man could spit on the floor out here in the 'office,' but not in the bunkhouse or the ranch house — Ma's orders.

"Mind them giant ravens over on South Fork? You know, them big black crows, boss?"

"What about 'em?"

"They kin get the scent of somethin' dead right off. They're worse than buzzards. Well, I done seen them circlin', back in the hills. I rid that way and found a dead hoss."

"You did? What brand did he pack?"

"He was thet hoss you sold to Doc Jones right after he come here. Well, somebody had shot him."

"Legs okay?"

"I looked his carcass over good, boss. No legs busted. Got me stumped. Boot marks around, and some empty .30-30 cartridges. Looked like some fightin' had gone on around there."

Mike Endicott frowned. "What does it read up to you, Scott?"

"Well, Doc Jeff rode into town on a ol' mare he'd borrowed from Clay Simmons. Said he had to shoot his hoss because he fell an' busted a pin. But thet dead hoss had no busted laigs, boss."

"Maybe he had a gunfight with somebody and his horse got killed?"

"Never found no dead man, or grave."

"Odd, eh? Well, keep your eyes open, Scott, and your rifle handy."

"I'll do that, Mike."

Mike Endicott leaned back in his swivel chair. He did not want trouble with the farmers. But if they brought trouble to him ... He loved the Quarter Circle U. He had fought and starved and worked his fingers to the bone to build his spread. He had fought the Sioux and killed the buffalo, and he had trailed in Oregon cattle. Now he was losing it all. Everything was going — his cattle, his range. Bankruptcy was facing him. All because of a blackleg germ — a germ he was accused of getting planted on this Scrub Pine grass.

Then his wife and Ray entered.

Strange, Ma held Ray by the hand, and he was a big kid now.

"What do you two want?"

Ma hesitated, and Ray looked up at her. Because of the dusk, Mike could not clearly see their faces.

Ma said, "Dad, we have something to tell you."

"More bad news, eh?"

"No, not bad news, Dad. Just promise us you won't fly off the handle?"

"That ain't fair, Clara. But I promise, anyway. You in on this too, Ray?"

"Yeah. I helped vaccinate the bull."

"You what?"

Ma Endicott said, "Ray let the cat out of the bag. Doc Jones left a vaccination needle and some vaccine with us. We vaccinated the bull right after he left. We were afraid to tell you."

"We had to save that bull," Ray said defensively. "He's got good blood and will produce good calves. You paid a high price for him."

Mike Endicott finally gained control of himself. "So you two did that — and saved the bull — and all the while I shoot off my big mug in front of Doc Jones that the bull didn't have blackleg — wrong diagnosis. Gawd, what a idiot I am!"

"Are you angry?"

"No, I'm not mad. I'm jes' ashamed of myself fer the way I treated Doc Jones. I'm glad you told me afore I went on makin' a fool out of myself again aroun' Doc."

Ray breathed deeply. "Man, am I happy! Ma, you stay here with Dad. I don't wanna see a woman bawl." The boy ran out, bare feet scampering.

Ma Endicott, apron to her eyes, moved in on Mike, who stood up and put his arms around her. Her heavy shoulders shook.

"Mike, we're losing everything — this blackleg is bankrupting us, Mike! Oh, if only Doc could get vaccine."

"Who stole his vaccine? If we knew whether or not it had been destroyed — If we could find where it is cached — "

"Wheeler and Osborne — they're behind it all. They want to drive you broke and break the farmers so they can get their deeds."

"I oughta kill them."

She stepped back and said, "Don't talk that way. You boast about taking the law into Scrub Pine. Now you talk about breaking down all you built up."

"There are times — "

"This is not one of those times!"

They stood there, two people facing middle age. Blackleg — the dread range disease — was breaking them. Years of work, hope, sweat, and play were slipping away. Yet, in this moment, they were bound tightly together, man and wife, each dependent on the other.

"Doc must figure I'm a bullheaded ol' sap. Well, I am at that! I crowed in Doc's face about thet bull. And Doc didn't tell me he had given you an'

243

Ray vaccine. He was too much of a gentleman. And look at the mess I got him in! I got him right in the middle of this range war, and just because he is a vet he has to take all the guff. Somebody even shot his hoss out from under him today."

"They what?"

"Keep this under your hat, and I'll tell you."

He told her what Scott had told him about finding the dead horse back on the ridge.

"Somebody tried to murder Doc. Ambush, prob'ly. Then, while this varmint was tryin' to kill him, another one climbed up on that freight wagon and stole the box of vaccine."

"That's logical."

"I'm headin' for town to apologize to Doc Jeff. I jes' cain't set here an' fume. Doc might be able to get more vaccine from Denver or Cheyenne. An' when the next batch comes in, the Quarter Circle U is goin' to guard it until it gets needled into sick critters."

From outside came Ray's voice. "Safe to come in now?"

"I want you to ride to town with me, Son."

Soon father and son were in saddle, heading for Scrub Pine. Mike questioned the youth about blackleg vaccine, how it was made and what it did to a sick critter. Mike Endicott knew a little about it, but Ray knew less.

"Can a person make vaccine, Son?"

"I don't know nothin' about vaccine. Doc Jones'll know. Doc Jeff is smart. Ma says so."

They loped toward town, following the wagon road. Dust puffed up behind their broncs' hoofs. Mike Endicott wondered just how hard it would be to apologize to Doc Jeff.

They topped a ridge, and about a mile ahead of them was the town of Scrub Pine, its cottonwood trees glistening in the setting sun. Then they were going down the slant, heading for the cow town.

Ray said, "Smoke in town, Dad.

Somethin' burnin', you reckon?"

"Looks to me like quite a bit of smoke, too. Probably burnin' some rubbish, I guess. The Merc burns up a lot of crates directly after it unpacks what is brought in on the freight wagon."

Ray scowled boyishly. "Seems like a mite of smoke, Dad."

A rider came toward them, bronc running hard. They watched him come closer, dust marking his progress.

Ray said, "That's Smoky, ain't it?"

"Looks like that pinto hoss of his. He aim to kill that hoss, ridin' him so hard? Headin' for the home ranch. Hey, Smoky!"

Smoky pulled in his bronc, face sweaty and grimy. "Boss, they's a fire down in town. Doc Jones's office an' lab'r'tory is goin' up in flames!"

"What caused the fire, Smoky?"

"Nobody knows. One minute the thing was all right; next, flame jus' busted outa the buildin' from all seams!"

"Doc in it?"

"Nobody was in it. Some of his chemicals must've exploded or caught on fire by themselves, or somethin'."

"Gawd Almighty, what's gonna happen next on this poor range?"

"Let's git ridin'," Ray said, loping ahead, quirt working.

15

"I SHOT down his hoss," Lee Osborne said. "The distance was too far for rifle work. He danged near winged me."

"Did he see you to recognize you?"

"No. I'm sure of that, Matt."

"You bungled the whole setup. You could have killed him and buried him out there, and nobody would ever have found his body. As it is, he comes into town, big as life, on an ol' plug."

"But the vaccine — You got the vaccine, Matt. And nobody saw you. That's what counts, Matt. You gettin' the vaccine. Matt, give me a shot, please, Matt?"

"You never earned a shot."

"I know I muffed things. But gimme a shot, Matt, and the next time I get a chance, this vet'll be dead. I promise that, Matt."

Matt Wheeler stood by the broken window, looking out on Scrub Pine's main street. Some of the farmers were in town. They were talking fight talk. They had backtrailed the freight wagon, but had found no tracks pointing to the place where Matt Wheeler, slipping out of the tall brush, could have come in behind the wagon and taken down the box of vaccine.

The farmers had come in to buy rifles and cartridges. They were spending all their money on ammunition and firearms. And when it was over, some of them would be dead. Their deeds would go to Matt Wheeler for a few cents on the dollar. He would finally have what he wanted.

Wheeler went to the safe and got Osborne's reward. Hidden behind the curtain that ran across the back part of the office, Lee Osborne hurriedly rolled up his sleeve, glee on his face. The needle went into the scarred forearm.

"Wonder if Doc Jeff saw me come

in behind that wagon?" Matt Wheeler asked.

Osborne pulled the needle free. "He never saw you. He was in a hollow duckin' my bullets. I feel better now. I could whup my weight in wildcats right now, Matt. Thanks."

Wheeler restored the needle to the safe, slammed the door, and twirled the knob, the lock making little clicks. Boots sounded out in the office proper.

"I'll stay here and listen," Osborne whispered.

Wheeler went into the office. A farmer had come in, wanting to borrow twenty dollars. Wheeler hemmed and hawed, finally giving in — taking a note. He gave a bit of advice, too.

"You farmers — don't move against the Endicott spread! They'll kill you — some of you. Even the winner will lose."

"Are we supposed to tuck tail and run, Wheeler? You're fightin' Endicott. We can fight him, too. An' whup him, too."

"Olaf, you're a little drunk. Don't do anything rash."

"We gotta fight, Matt."

The farmer left, unsteady on his feet. Wheeler grinned at Osborne, who had come out from behind the curtain. Osborne settled against the wall, feeling the heat come into his blood. "The fools, Matt — they believe you!"

"People are stupid, Lee."

Another farmer came in. He boned forty bucks off Wheeler. "Wonder where the heck Endicott has hid thet vaccine he stole off'n thet freight wagon?"

Wheeler was sly. "Maybe Endicott didn't steal it, Martin."

"If he didn't, he had one of his hands do it."

"Maybe Doc Jeff didn't order vaccine."

The farmer looked at him with bloodshot eyes. "What do you mean by that, Wheeler? I don't foller you."

"Maybe the box didn't contain vaccine. Maybe Doc Jeff just said it did. We don't know for sure."

"Doc ain't no liar."

"You don't know that, either."

The farmer rubbed a whiskery jaw. "Only thing I know is that the Quarter Circle U has took in blackleg to break us farmers." He left, boots wicked on the plank sidewalk.

"More propaganda," Osborne said dryly.

"World exists on it," Wheeler said. He regarded the jagged edges of the broken window, and the memory of its deliberate breakage came to him, rankling him. "All right — so far, so good. What if the vet can make vaccine?"

"Can he do that?"

"He might be able to. Some of the farmers have mentioned that possibility. I'll scout around."

"I'll stay here, Matt."

Wheeler went from store to store, from saloon to saloon, listening and adding a few words, stoking the fires of hate in a subtle manner. One farmer, he found out, had gone back to his farm.

"He's gonna bring in a sick yearlin' heifer, Matt. Heifer has got blackleg. Bringin' her into Doc's office, he is."

"Why?"

"Doc says he'll make some vaccine, or at least try. Reckon it's made outa the blood of a stricken cow, they tell me."

Wheeler nodded. He knew a little bit about vaccine — how it acted, how it was manufactured.

"The manufacture of blackleg vaccine, they tell me, is a patented process. If Doc makes some, he can go to the clink."

"He mentioned that. But he aims to try, anyway. He might be able to make some. It's our only chance, seein' Endicott swiped thet other vaccine off'n the freight wagon."

Wheeler listened, pondered, then returned to his office. Lee Osborne smoked a cigarette that had a peculiar odor. His eyes were aglow with wicked purpose.

"I oughta kill thet pill-roller, Matt."

"Why?"

"Git rid of him for once an for all."

"Then you'd be tried for murder unless you killed him from ambush. You tried that today. You failed. Do we fear the doc, or do we fear his knowledge?"

"Me, I don't fear him one inch."

"All right, I'll put it this way. Doc has nothing he can use against us except his brain. What we really have to fight is the products of his brain, not him as a man."

"That's right."

Wheeler told about the plan to make vaccine. Osborne's eyes glistened.

"Can he make vaccine, Matt?"

"I think he can." Wheeler stretched a few points deliberately. "If he makes vaccine, we're whipped."

"I'll burn down his office! With it an' his lab'r'tory supplies gone, he sure cain't make no vaccine!"

Wheeler said, "By gosh, that's right!"

He had gained his point. But he had permitted Lee Osborne the privilege of stating it. The man had pride, and he had deliberately led Osborne to this conclusion.

Osborne studied him. "Where is Doc now?"

"In the Branding Iron. Him and the farmers are waiting. You could go down the alley, break a back window, sprinkle the inside with kerosene."

"I got a gallon of kerosene, too. You go to the cafe and watch Doc and the farmers, eh?"

"All right."

Osborne went out the back door, and Wheeler went up the street, where he met Old Man Dial.

"Where is your friend, the vet?" Wheeler asked.

"Brandin' Iron."

"Take it easy," Wheeler said.

Things were working out correctly. Maybe it was best that Osborne had not murdered the vet. The vet was well liked. Even the talk about his

255

being the possible killer of George Miller was dying down.

The Branding Iron was jammed. Farmers sat on stools, and in booths. Wheeler took a place behind Doc Jones, who sat toward the front of the cafe. He ordered coffee from Millie, then said to the vet, "Heard of your plan to manufacture vaccine. Think you can do it, Doc?"

Doc Jones smiled. "I can try. Beyond that, I promise nothing."

"The process, so I understand, is patented, is it not?"

Doc Jeff nodded. "Cattle are dying. If I can make vaccine and save them, to blazes with all the patents!"

Wheeler nodded seriously. "Good way to feel. Hope you're successful."

"If I can make it, so much the better. I might get fined or make the clink, but I might save some cattle, too."

Wheeler nodded. "You make some vaccine for us farmers, and we'll see you don't get fined or go to jail, Doc." He appealed to the farmers. "Ain't that so, boys? We'll stick by Doc Jeff. How about it?"

"He's our only hope!"

"That's right, Matt."

"You said it, Wheeler!"

"He won't pay a fine or go to jail. If he does, I'll be dead."

Wheeler said, "You got them behind you, and that is what we want. We don't want trouble; we want peace. I wonder if Endicott really stole your vaccine?"

"I'll bet he did," Barclay growled.

Doc Jones said, "We can't prove anything, Barclay." By now, he knew that Barclay was only a troublemaker, probably stationed in the farmers ranks by Wheeler and Osborne to stir up trouble.

Jones said nothing. He had his own theories about who had stolen the vaccine and who had tried to kill him back in the brush. He looked at Millie and winked. She winked back. Doc Jeff, young and healthy, felt very happy over that subtle feminine wink.

"Doc can make vaccine," a farmer declared. "I can feel it in my bones."

Doc Jeff said, "You have more confidence in me than I have in myself."

Millie said, "More coffee and doughnuts, men? Hold out your cups."

She was pouring coffee when the back door suddenly opened and Old Man Dial pushed into the room.

"Doc Jeff, your lab is on fire!"

For a moment, the effect was one of stunned disbelief. Then Doc Jones tore out the door and stopped. The old man was right. Smoke and fire poured from every corner of his office-laboratory. Evidently, the entire interior was burning.

Behind him, farmers boiled out, stunned and afraid. They stood for a moment in the street, staring at the flames.

"Can you make vaccine now?"

"Not with my lab gone. Even the formula for it is in there. We gotta get that fire out, men!"

Matt Wheeler immediately took command. "Get buckets from the stores and houses! Then line up and start a bucket brigade. You, get there — get in line, men. Here comes some buckets."

At this moment, a cowpuncher ran out of the Golden Dollar Saloon across the street. Hurriedly, he untied a Quarter Circle U horse, flanked the bronc around, hit his stirrup with a boot, and rode madly out of town.

"He might've set it on fire," a farmer hollered. "He's a Endicott man, an' he's leavin' town in a hurry — "

Wheeler snarled, "You might have somethin' there, fella!"

Deputy Sheriff Coogan took over. They had no chance to save the lab, he said, but they had to save the rest of town. Jeff got into the bucket line, and Millie stood beside him, passing the filled buckets to him — a difficult job for a little woman.

"You'd best get in the other line,

Millie. It handles the empty buckets coming back."

"I want to be with you, Jeff."

"Thanks," he said, and meant it.

"How do you figure it started, Jeff?"

"I don't know. I think it was set on fire." He closed his mouth then, for he had a plan, and it was best not to tip his hand. "Anyway, I certainly can't make vaccine now."

The fire burned savagely. There was hardly any wind, so this helped keep the fire from spreading. Men and women worked with desperate purpose. Buckets came back empty, returned to the fire filled with water. They were then doused on the flames.

Millie said, "There's Mike Endicott, and his boy is with him."

One farmer growled, "Sure as shootin' it is. Wonder why he always shows up at times like this? Mebbe he done set this on fire!"

"Talk sense," Doc Jeff warned angrily.

Endicott got in line below Doc Jeff. "Smoky met us as we came into town,

Jeff, and told us about the fire. I sent him to the ranch to get the boys in to help. What caused it, do you know?"

"We don't know."

"Heard you aimed to make blackleg vaccine, too."

"I was going to try. I don't know how successful that try would have been, though. Now it's all out of the question."

"Tough luck, Doc Jeff. That vaccine sure saved that bull."

Doc Jeff gave the man a look. "What bull?"

"The one out to my spread, of course. Ma an' Ray tol' me about vaccinatin' him. I'm real sorry about the way I acted an' what I said, Doc Jeff."

Doc Jeff grinned. "Glad you came around, Mike. But you'll have to work it out alone, 'cause when this fire is over, I'm leavin' Scrub Pine for good."

"Leavin' for good?"

"What will I have to keep me here?"

Doc Jones noticed that Millie was listening. "My office gone, no trade, no vaccine, and cattle dying. I've had nothing but tough luck since I came here. I'm leaving while I'm all in one piece."

Matt Wheeler heard it, too. "Doc, talk sense. We need you."

"You don't need me. I'm no good without a laboratory or vaccine. And I can't get vaccine, either. Closest is Denver, and that's a week or ten days away. No, I'm drifting, men."

They worked steadily. Farmers glared at Endicott, who glared back at them. Gradually, the flames receded. The danger of the fire's spreading to other buildings became remote. The walls fell in, cascading sparks, and then they were pouring water on burning embers, changing them to ashes. And the fire was a thing of the past. So was Doc Jones's laboratory and so were the hopes of the farmers — and of Mike Endicott, too.

Doc Jeff said, "No use your riders

comin' into town, Mike. The fire is out. These farmers are touchy against you. They figure you stole that vaccine off the wagon."

"They lie."

"Sure they do. But they might get into trouble with your hands. Ride out and turn them back, please."

"Okay."

Young Ray offered a boyish hand. "I'll sure miss you, Doc Jeff." He could say no more. He turned and ran for his horse, climbing hurriedly into the saddle.

"You're a hero to him," Millie said.

Doc Jeff nodded.

"Now his hero is running," she added.

He looked at her. "What else can I do?"

"Stay and fight, of course."

He spread out grimy hands. "Fight without anything to fight with — or for? Millie, I'm no fool. I know when I'm whipped."

"Are you a coward?"

"Call it what you want. I call it plain good sense." They had stopped in front of a saloon. "I don't want a drink. Nothing would taste good to me. I'm without a rifle, a cartridge, or a roll of blankets. I've only got my horse and saddle . . . and my future."

"Your future!" she scoffed. "You're no man! You're a — "

Doc Jeff smiled. "I'll be seeing you later," he said, and left her.

16

THAT night, Doc Jones made camp back in the brush on the ridge beyond the county seat — Highring. He staked out his pack horse and rode into town. When he had last seen Millie Simmons and Matt Wheeler, Jeff had had no rifle. Now a Winchester .30-30 rode in his saddle holster.

He went from saloon to saloon, wandering aimlessly. He kept his mouth shut and his ears open. He met the train, but only a woman got off. When he had first arrived, he had gone to the depot and collected two telegrams. One said that blackleg vaccine was being sent up from Denver. That was from the wholesale house that had shipped out the stolen box of vaccine. But it would take a week for the vaccine to reach Scrub Pine.

He slept in the brush that night; the next day he returned to Highring. Again he met the train. Two men got off, carrying saddles, and with them were two women, evidently their wives. Doc Jeff felt a touch of disappointment. He went to a saloon and ordered a beer he did not want.

Down the bar, sipping a lemonade, was a bony, slender man of middle age; his eyes met those of Doc Jones. The man looked back at his drink, talked a while with the bartender, and left the saloon.

Doc Jeff asked, "Who's that button?"

"Stranger around here."

Doc Jeff, through the big window, saw the stranger come out of a store, a gunny sack over his shoulder. Supplies, probably. The man mounted a trail-toughened black horse at the hitch rack after tying the sack behind his saddle. He rode out of Highring then, his bronc at a running walk. Doc Jeff saw the handle of a Winchester protruding from the man's saddle holster and read the brand on the horse: Rocking Chair Bar. It was a strange brand to him.

Within ten minutes, Doc Jeff Jones also left Highring and rode south. Ahead, rim-rock stretched, bleak and barren, marked by scrub pine and cedar. Doc Jones headed back to his camp. He was squatting by a small fire, roasting the thighs of a cottontail rabbit on a wire, when he heard the brush move behind him.

"Come on in," he said without turning around.

Boots moved closer, and the stranger stood beside him. "Supper time," the stranger said. "That rabbit smells good, Doc Jones."

Doc Jeff looked at the man. "You're from the attorney general's office, like the telegram said?"

"I don't follow you. You got any identification?"

Smiling a little, Jeff dug for his wallet. "Here is my card from the veterinarian's state association."

The man looked at the picture, then

at Doc Jones. "I'm Henry," he said. "Just Henry. No last name. The boss sent me out in response to your first telegram. I cut across country. I like a horse and hate a train."

"I have been watching the trains."

"What's the deal, Doc Jeff?"

"I'm on the lam. Told them I was leaving for good so you and I could work in private and on the q.t. What do you know about them?"

"Quite a bit."

"Like what, for instance?"

The man smiled. "I'm hungry right now. How about a leg of that cottontail? Then we can talk and outline a plan."

Doc Jeff said, "Sure, Henry. I've got a .30-30." He patted the weapon as it lay beside him. "Had to steal it." He told Henry the rifle had belonged to Millie Simmons.

Later, the Winchester rifle leaned against a sandstone ledge high on the rim-rock that overlooked Scrub Pine.

Doc Jones said, "I'd best move that rifle; it might reflect the sun and give away our hiding place."

"Good idea, Jeff."

Jeff picked up the Winchester and showed a twisted smile. "Millie will miss this rifle and wonder where it went to. Sure wish I could see her." He squatted, back to a boulder, and rubbed his whiskery jaw. He looked at the man called Henry, who sat with his back against a rock, field glasses on the dust beside him.

Jeff said, "Those two are tough men. They won't give up without a fight. I never knew they were killers until you told me."

"I've trailed a lot of them, Jeff. A weary job."

Henry took off his hat and let the wind cool his forehead.

Doc Jeff nodded, waiting.

"Ever since I was sixteen, I've worked on the side of the law. I've hunted them down, killed them, put them behind bars. They never win. Some fight, some cave in. The meek ones sometimes fight like tigers, and the guys with the big mouths cave in when the chips are down."

Doc Jeff said nothing.

Henry's eyes touched him. "What's your plan, Doc Jeff? You know this deal better than I do."

"We could arrest them, but that wouldn't show us where the vaccine is. We need that vaccine, and need it bad."

"Once a vet, always a vet."

Doc Jeff smiled, but he felt awful. He was dirty to the skin and he needed a shave, and the ground was not a spring mattress when it came to sleeping.

"Cattle need that vaccine, Henry."

"Maybe they broke it. Opened the box and smashed the bottles. That's logical, isn't it?"

"I doubt it. They wouldn't take the trouble, for one thing. It was done in a hurry. I think that Matt Wheeler might have just buried it. Or even cached it somewhere."

Henry nodded. "Say he hid it somewhere . . . We want him to go to it, and then we can jump him and his partner. So far, so good — but how can we get him to ride out to the vaccine?"

"I got a plan."

Doc Jeff outlined his plan. Henry nodded, then said, "It all depends on this uncle of your girl's, eh? This farmer named Clay Simmons?"

"That's it, Henry."

"We'd best get to work."

With Doc Jeff carrying the Winchester, they went to their broncs. It was dark when they rode into the yard of Clay Simmons' farm. The dog's barking brought the farmer to the door, rifle in hand.

"Doc Jones, Clay. And a friend."

The farmer was surprised to see the veterinarian. "Thought you'd pulled out. Millie is danged near mad down in town. What's on your mind?"

"We got a plan, and we want your help."

The farmer looked at one man, then the other. "I'd be sure proud to help you, Doc Jeff, seein' you're goin' be a member of my family . . . after you marry Millie."

"If I live that long, Clay."

"Shoot, Doc Jeff."

"Have you lost any cattle due to blackleg?"

The farmer frowned. "No, not a head yet, Doc Jeff. Only reason is, I'm so far to my lonesome, I guess, and no cows have brought the disease in on this section of soil. Why ask?"

"I want you to ride to town tomorrow. Act mysterious, act like you're purty drunk, and hint about havin' some blackleg vaccine, that you have vaccinated your cows on the sly."

"Them farmers are already accusin' me of havin' you slip vaccine into my cows. They don't like me too well. What's behind all this, anyway?"

Henry looked at Doc Jeff. "Is he honest?"

"I think he is."

"Then tell him about it."

Doc Jeff talked at some length with Millie's uncle. He agreed to the plan and left for town within the hour. Just as he was turning his old gray horse, Doc Jeff said, "Get the impression over to Wheeler and Osborne that you have found where they cached the vaccine."

"What if they didn't hide it? What if they busted the bottles?"

Doc Jeff's jaw tightened. "We got to chance that."

"I'll do my best!"

The farmer loped toward town. Doc Jones and Henry again headed back into the rough country. From the rimrock, they could see the lamplight in the farmhouses and at the Quarter Circle U outfit.

"If the farmers really move against Endicott, there'll be trouble, Henry."

"The sheriff is watching it, they tell me. This deputy of yours — Coogan — is workin' closely with the sheriff, so your friend the attorney general told me. We get these rats cornered, and a lot of dirty linen will be washed.

We make camp tonight around where you got the horse shot out from under you, eh?"

"That's the point where the vaccine was stolen. And unless I guess wrong, it's somewhere around that spot — unless, of course, they broke it up. Lots of *ifs*, Henry."

"Life is full of them, Jeff."

They picketed their horses and rolled blankets on the hard ground. Henry went to sleep immediately. Doc Jeff did some thinking, hands behind his head, as he looked at the Montana stars.

Wheeler's scheme was surprising in its cold-bloodedness. Information given him by Henry had thrown new facets of light onto it. Had their plan worked, the pair would have been worth a million dollars — after they had gotten the deeds to Scrub Pine land.

* * *

Doc Jeff had slept sitting up, his back against a rock. He was lying on his

274

side smoking a cigarette when Henry woke up.

"Be another hot day," he said.

Doc Jeff nodded, then ground out his cigarette. "Now, where could they have hidden this vaccine? We've looked for days and found nothing. If they broke the bottles, we should see some glass around, vaccine spilled."

"This is a mighty big country."

"Maybe they got it cached in town?"

"I doubt it. You said the window was busted in Wheeler's office. Anybody could get in there anytime he wanted. And besides, somebody might have seen them tote it into town, for the box is pretty big, you say."

"That's right."

"We'll find something, Doc Jeff. Patience is what counts in this game. Patience and work. We did right in sending Clay Simmons to town. I got a hunch we're on the right track."

"Let's hope you're right."

Henry built a little fire and made bacon and eggs and coffee. Below them was the wagon road connecting Highring and Scrub Pine.

They spent the day in the rocks. Through field glasses, Doc Jones watched Big Mike Endicott ride range. Quarter Circle U cattle were down; many carcasses dotted the hills and gullies. The day passed slowly. A thousand ideas came and went, a thousand fears plagued him.

Maybe their plan had failed. Maybe Clay Simmons had not been able to convey the impression that he had found the stolen vaccine and had vaccinated his cattle. Maybe, maybe, maybe!

Night found them still on the rimrock. No riders rode the trail that night. The range land was quiet, not broken by the movements of men on horseback. A few coyotes talked to the moon; a bull bawled in the distance — another victim of blackleg.

The stage came rocking in, heading for Scrub Pine. Then it went back, horses moving through the dawn.

They spent another forenoon on the rim-rock. Doc Jeff watched through field glasses. About three o'clock two riders left Scrub Pine, heading toward the county seat. They had to ride the road almost under the rim-rock ledge.

The field glasses showed them clearly. Matt Wheeler, arrogant, domineering, big — riding in the lead, sorrel pushing through the heat. And behind him rode Lee Osborne.

Doc Jeff said, "There they are, Henry!"

Henry was a cat, coming instantly to his senses. He was rigid and did not move, for movement might expose him and give away their hideout.

"Who, Doc Jeff?"

Doc Jeff handed him the field glasses. "Wheeler and Osborne," he said.

Henry crawled to the rim-rock ledge on his belly and focused the glasses on the two riders.

"They're turning up a draw there in the lava beds, Doc Jeff. Ridin' east, after leavin' the road." He became thoughtful, and Doc Jeff Jones saw his lips harden. "So they are the two we have to kill, or put behind bars for life."

"We swing in behind them?" Doc Jeff asked.

"That we do."

They went for their broncs. And the man called Henry lifted his whiskery face to the sun.

"And we thought the wolves would hit at night."

"Better this time of day. We can see better."

Wheeler and Osborne were riding away from them, going deeper into the canyon.

"Maybe Clay Simmons played his part well, eh, Doc Jeff?"

"Looks like it," the veterinarian said slowly.

Henry looked at him, and his mouth showed a bitter smile. "We close in for the kill," he said tonelessly.

Unseen by Wheeler or Osborne, Doc Jeff and the manhunter rode off the rim-rock. And the sun, slanting in with savage brightness, glistened on the polished stock of the Winchester .30-30 rifle in the saddle boot of Doc Jeff Jones.

17

"A USELESS ride," Matt Wheeler was saying quietly. "The vaccine is right where I buried it, Lee. Over under those rocks in that sand. You can scarcely see the marks left by my shovel 'cause the wind has howled through here and leveled off the sand."

Osborne nodded, leaning forward, weight creaking on saddle leather. "There might not be a box buried there, Matt. He could have dug it up and then refilled the hole with sand again."

"He has no vaccine."

"You think he's lyin'?"

"Sure Simmons is lying. Making up things because he's drunk. After we drag that cowhide across his range, his cattle will die, too. He's just isolated, and we haven't paid enough attention to him."

Osborne rubbed his jaw thoughtfully. "But what would he gain by makin' up such a story, Matt?"

"I don't know. Just the rambling words of a drunken man, I guess."

Osborne shook his head. "Seems to me like they's somethin' behin' his words," he said. He dismounted and untied the short-handled spade from his saddle. "We'll see for sure, right pronto."

Matt Wheeler leaned against the fork of his saddle, thinking that this was a lonesome and dreary spot. Not enough grass to keep even a jackrabbit. The wind talked against the higher igneous rocks, causing a thin and high whistle that was enough to make a man nervous.

Suddenly he asked, "Did I hear something, Lee?"

Osborne stopped digging. He wiped his forehead and grinned. "You heard my spade hittin' wood, Matt. The box must be there yet. I'm gonna get enough dirt off it so I can look into it. He might jus' have taken out the vaccine and left the box buried. He ain't no simpleton, thet farmer."

"Let's check fast, then get out of here."

Osborne's dull eyes held faint amusement. "You sound ringy, Matt."

"I am spooky — spooky as a four-year-old bronc that smells a she-bear in the wind."

He dismounted, taking his Winchester out of its saddle boot, then walked over to where Lee Osborne knelt and ripped loose a board on top of the box. Suddenly Matt Wheeler turned, rifle rising.

Osborne froze, looking up at his boss. "What is it, Matt?"

"I thought I heard something."

Osborne cocked his head, hands on his rifle. He listened and then said, "Only the wind in the high rocks. We got ragged nerves, Matt."

"Osborne! Over there — a man!"

Osborne was pulled to his boots by the stern magnet of Matt Wheeler's voice. He dropped his rifle, and both hands came back and found the black handles of his guns.

Osborne's lips moved. "Doc Jones, eh?"

Wheeler cocked his rifle. Sanity had returned, and his eyes became narrowed. The clicking of the Winchester's hammer was sharp and keen. But the voice of Matt Wheeler was now natural again — husky and deep.

"Doc Jones, eh? Comin' outa the rocks like a ghost. How come you wander around these lava beds at a time like this, hoss quack?"

Doc Jones held a Winchester .30-30. "Trailed you out from town," he said. "Clay Simmons and I worked out a deal to pull you boys to your loot. The jig is up for you two killers."

Osborne wet his lips, his eyes shifty. "Killers?"

Doc Jeff lifted his voice, but his gaze was still tied to the two men who stood there watching him with cat-quick eyes.

"Come out of the brush, Henry."

Henry emerged from a clump of buckbrush. He did not carry his Winchester, but he had his hands on his holstered .45's. Osborne looked at him, and Osborne's hands started to shake.

"Who are you?" Wheeler asked, studying him.

Henry said, "I'm a special agent out of the territorial office of the attorney general. Doc Jeff notified his old friend, the attorney general, and he got me on this case."

"Case?" Wheeler's voice was a little strained.

Doc Jeff watched Osborne. The man was shaking slightly, and the killer lust was on him. It lay across his shoulders, in his eyes, in the set of his mouth. Doc Jeff wet his lips, but his tongue was bone dry. A muscle in his neck, held too long under tension, started to jerk, then stopped.

He heard Henry's controlled voice saying, "We did some investigating,

Wheeler. You two killed a banker in Big Pine, Arizona Territory. You also robbed the U.S. mails in Arizona."

"You talk like a fool, stranger. You've got us confused with somebody else. We'll go to court and prove you're wrong."

"You'll go to court, but your goose is cooked," Henry went on. "We even know about that oil geologist in Denver. He's in the clink now, on the charge of helping you two skinflint these farmers."

Lee Osborne had stopped shaking. "Matt, what'll we do?" he said.

"Go with them, of course." Wheeler turned and held out his rifle, apparently to surrender, and Lee Osborne screamed, "I'll die before I hang!" And then, without warning, Matt Wheeler was on one knee, his Winchester rising. And his hoarse voice croaked, "Get them, Lee! Kill them!"

It happened with terrible suddenness. A gesture of surrender suddenly changed to one of warfare. Doc Jones, rifle rising, saw the sudden lift of Osborne's black guns, saw the .45's start over the holsters, muzzles rising. He shot without raising his rifle to his shoulder, and sent his bullet against Lee Osborne's right shoulder.

The .30-30 slug drove Osborne around, making him drop his right-hand gun. Doc Jeff moved in, aware of the roar caused by the guns of Wheeler and Henry, and his rifle came down, hard and solid. The barrel smashed across Osborne's forehead, ripping hide loose; it knocked him to the sand, where he lay unconscious.

Doc Jeff turned, rifle raised. His eyes took in the scene instantly. Henry was against the far boulders; he had lost his rifle. He was sagging there, knees starting to buckle, and Doc Jones almost looked into Matt Wheeler's rifle.

The thought came to the veterinarian that Wheeler would kill him. And, in that same moment, he thought of Millie Simmons. He saw Wheeler's face, ugly and twisted and bloody, leering as the rifle raised. Wheeler was bunched, a solid mass of muscle, a killer to the core.

Afterward, it was not clear to Doc Jeff, but he remembered hearing Wheeler's Winchester roar. Then his own rifle kicked back, solid and good, and the bullet found Wheeler.

Wheeler said something, but Doc Jeff could not remember the words, for surprise was with him, and with it a great sense of happiness. Wheeler, in his haste, had missed! That was all that counted!

Wheeler dropped his Winchester. He walked ahead, put one hand out, and balanced himself against a rock. He looked down at Osborne's prone body, and his lips moved. This time, the vet heard the land-locater's words:

"I'll be with you, Lee . . . in a minute or two."

Wheeler stood there, looking at Osborne. Doc Jeff had his eyes on the man, and he was aware of Henry moving toward him. Then Wheeler looked at Doc Jeff, but his eyes were already dead — sick and tired and without hope.

Then, without a word, Wheeler's knees broke, and he lay on the sand beside Lee Osborne. He lay on his belly, his face in the hole Osborne had dug.

Doc Jeff looked at Henry. "He shot you, Henry?"

"Right through the thigh. Knocked me back and almost put me out of commission. Did you kill Osborne, Doc Jeff?"

"Knocked him cold."

Odd, how distant his voice sounded, how dull it was. Was it his voice? And the heart inside him — would it leap through his ribs?

Henry sat down. "I hear horses somewhere, Doc. Down the canyon."

Doc Jones heard the hoof sounds, too. The thought came that perhaps Wheeler and Osborne had confederates coming. Then this thought was ruled out as a familiar voice called, "Hey, where are you?"

Doc Jeff said, "Voice of Mike Endicott," and hollered, "This way, Mike!"

They came roaring around the corner, then their broncs skidded to a stop. Mike Endicott and Clay Simmons swung down, full of questions. Behind them, farmers and cowboys sat horses. Millie Simmons was with them, too.

She said, "Clay told me all about it. We went out to get the help of the Quarter Circle U bunch. The farmers and the cowboys are friends. But how are *you*, Doc?"

Doc Jeff found a smile. "I'm all right . . . since you arrived, honey."

★ ★ ★

Within six months, the first oil derrick was in Scrub Pine. Oil was hit at a very short depth on the Clay Simmons' farm. Scrub Pine was no longer a small town; it was soon bigger than the county seat.

Vaccine had put blackleg out of business.

Rancher Mike Endicott, almost ruined by the savage work of Wheeler and Osborne, filed on a homestead, as did his wife and the older members of his family. Quarter Circle U cowpunchers also filed on homesteads to get in on the oil boom.

The man named Henry, called to another job at the far end of the territory, left Scrub Pine within three weeks. When he left, he promised to come back to the wedding of Doc Jeff Jones and Millie Simmons.

They had thrown Lee Osborne into jail and kept dope away from him until he had gone wild and had talked. But the law did not get to hang Osborne. Osborne, using his sheet as a hangman's rope, took his own life in his cell.

There was a big dance on the night Doc Jeff and Millie got married at Clay Simmons' farm. Cowboys danced with the wives and daughters of farmers. Ma

Endicott kissed Doc Jeff and peered up at him in her nearsighted manner.

"Remember when you had me and Ray vaccinate the bull, Doc Jeff?"

"I sure do, Ma."

"We sure pulled one over on Dad!"

Mike Endicott was rather drunk. He and Old Man Dial had cached a gallon of whiskey in a haystack down by the barn.

"You three sure ganged up on me," the rancher said.

The fiddle started, and the accordion made its noises. The caller hollered, "All get partners for the do-si-do."

Another dance started. Kerosene lamps sent out yellow rays. Boots and heavy shoes ground on the floor.

Doc Jeff slipped into the kitchen, where his bride was making supper. He came up behind her, put his arms around her thin waist, and kissed her on the neck.

"Ready to go, honey?"

"We'll sneak out soon."

"Only way we can get away."

They went out the back door. Doc Jeff had his buggy team tied to one of the big cottonwood trees. Soon they were moving across the prairie, moonlight brittle and clean over sagebrush and greasewood, moonlight that glistened on the new oil derrick.

The team jogged along, reins tied around the whip socket on the buggy's dashboard. Doc Jeff leaned back and looked at the sky.

"Beautiful, isn't it?"

"It sure is, honey."

He looked at Millie. "But you're more beautiful."

Moonlight showed tiny tears of happiness in her eyes. "I hope you think that way when I'm old and — "

"I sure will," Doc Jeff said throatily.

THE END

FIGHTING RAMROD
Charles N. Heckelmann

Most men would have cut their losses, but Frazer counted the bullets in his guns and said he'd soak the range in blood before he'd give up another inch of what was his.

LONE GUN
Eric Allen

Smoke Blackbird had been away too long. The Lequires had seized the Blackbird farm, forcing the Indians and settlers off, and no one seemed willing to fight! He had to fight alone.

THE THIRD RIDER
Barry Cord

Mel Rawlins wasn't going to let anything stand in his way. His father was murdered, his two brothers gone. Now Mel rode for vengeance.

ARIZONA DRIFTERS
W. C. Tuttle

When drifting Dutton and Lonnie Steelman decide to become partners they find that they have a common enemy in the formidable Thurston brothers.

TOMBSTONE
Matt Braun

Wells Fargo paid Luke Starbuck to outgun the silver-thieving stagecoach gang at Tombstone. Before long Luke can see the only thing bearing fruit in this eldorado will be the gallows tree.

HIGH BORDER RIDERS
Lee Floren

Buckshot McKee and Tortilla Joe cut the trail of a border tough who was running Mexican beef into Texas. They stopped the smuggler in his tracks.

BRETT RANDALL, GAMBLER
E. B. Mann

Larry Day had the choice of running away from the law or of assuming a dead man's place. No matter what he decided he was bound to end up dead.

THE GUNSHARP
William R. Cox

The Eggerleys weren't very smart. They trained their sights on Will Carney and Arizona's biggest blood bath began.

THE DEPUTY OF SAN RIANO
Lawrence A. Keating and
Al. P. Nelson

When a man fell dead from his horse, Ed Grant was spotted riding away from the scene. The deputy sheriff rode out after him and came up against everything from gunfire to dynamite.

FARGO: MASSACRE RIVER
John Benteen

The ambushers up ahead had now blocked the road. Fargo's convoy was a jumble, a perfect target for the insurgents' weapons!

SUNDANCE: DEATH IN THE LAVA
John Benteen

The Modoc's captured the wagon train and its cargo of gold. But now the halfbreed they called Sundance was going after it . . .

HARSH RECKONING
Phil Ketchum

Five years of keeping himself alive in a brutal prison had made Brand tough and careless about who he gunned down . . .

FARGO: PANAMA GOLD
John Benteen

With foreign money behind him, Buckner was going to destroy the Panama Canal before it could be completed. Fargo's job was to stop Buckner.

FARGO:
THE SHARPSHOOTERS
John Benteen

The Canfield clan, thirty strong were raising hell in Texas. Fargo was tough enough to hold his own against the whole clan.

PISTOL LAW
Paul Evan Lehman

Lance Jones came back to Mustang for just one thing — revenge! Revenge on the people who had him thrown in jail.